Cry of the Seals

J. Finn Wake

Lightning Source, Inc.

J. Finn Wake/Lightning Source, an imprint of IngramSpark
1246 Heil Quaker Blvd.
LaVergne, TN 37086
www.jfinnwake.com

Publisher's Note: This is a work of fiction. Names, characters, places, and incidents are a product of the author's imagination. Locales and public names are sometimes used for atmospheric purposes. Any resemblance to actual people, living or dead, or to businesses, companies, events, institutions, or locales is completely coincidental.

Book Layout & Design ©2017 - BookDesignTemplates.com
Cover Design: Tony Simerman

Cry of the Seals/ J. Finn Wake. -- 1st ed.
ISBN 978-0-9995473-0-4 (paperback)
ISBN: 978-0-9995473-1-1 (e-book)

This book is for all my family and friends who have followed me on this journey, and offered support along the way.

"The sea, once it casts its spell, holds one in its net of wonder forever."

– Jacques Cousteau

ACKNOWLEDGMENTS

Writing a novel is a complicated task and this project was no exception. Thank you to my fellow writers, Ashley Simerman, Kevin Weinert, and Nick Marnell who took the time to read this manuscript, offer valued suggestions, and push me in new directions. Special thanks to editor Wendy Tokunaga, who offered stellar suggestions and invaluable insight on how to proceed after the first iteration of this book, to Sean Abbey, who explained the differences between species of seals and sea lions, and offered specific feedback about the ocean and the creatures that live there, to my son, Jefferson, who offered his unique perspective to this novel, and to my husband, Dan, and other son, Jon, who put up with this craziness from inception to publication.

1.

"**G**o faster!" Noah screamed from the passenger seat. His mom shot him a warning glance, her knuckles white on the steering wheel, tires crunching on the pavement as they took the turn onto the main road of the tiny speck of the town of Klamath, just south of the Oregon border.

Noah rolled down his window and leaned out, trying to see past a large crowd that had formed on either side of the roadway. "Hurry!" Wind whipped his hair, trying to steal his voice. "They're in trouble, I know it!"

"I'm going as fast as I can, Noah. You want me to crash?"

"No, but—"

"Last time we went this fast it cost me close to three hundred dollars and a trip to the DMV for that Nothin' But Laughs comedy driving school . . . "

Oh no. The buzzing in Noah's head had started again.

". . . which was not funny at all, by the way."

He knew his mom was still talking, but he could barely understand the words she was saying. He could only watch her mouth move.

"Do you want to be . . . cause of your mother . . . through—"

Her voice became garbled. How could she talk that fast without taking a breath? Now his head felt fuzzy, filled with a weird pressure. Was he having a stroke? That's not possible, he thought. I'm only fifteen.

Towering redwoods flanked the road. Noah stifled a scream when his mom slowed the car to a crawl. He wanted to push her aside and stomp on the accelerator. Shafts of blinding sunlight cast smoky stripes along the cooking asphalt. "Go faster!"

The pressure increased in his head as they turned off toward the bridge, a crush of color along both sides of the roadway. Throngs of people pushed together in a seemingly liquid movement spilled off of the sidewalks. "Come on, come on," Noah muttered. Then the feeling in his head was gone. Just like that. He felt a sense of uncertainty.

Noah's mother guided the faded station wagon slowly through a large crowd. "Look at all these people. They're everywhere."

A bead of sweat trickled down Noah's neck, heightening his sense of dread. People of every age and size seemed to have converged on this one spot. The wave of pedestrians pulsed as children were lifted onto shoulders, parents intent on getting a better vantage point from the girded steel bridge traversing the Klamath River, intent on seeing the giant beasts below.

"There they are. I see them!" He pointed toward the blur of the river below where the two large gray masses hid just inches from the surface. "Stop. Let me out!" Not waiting for a response, he jumped out of the slowly moving car, the door hanging ajar as he ran off.

His mom yelled after him, but he was gone.

***

Noah's thick hair bounced as he ran toward the bridge, his long legs a blur as he tore through the crowd. A wall of people stood crushed near the railing; small children poked heads through the eight-inch slats to peer down at the slow ripples of green water. Onlookers perched themselves along the river's edge, colorful dots of anticipation.

"Hey, watch it, kid," a large man barked as Noah rushed past. The man wore a baseball cap with a plastic shark fin attached to the top. His flip-flops hung loose on his bulbous feet and his chest was covered with a loud, green T-shirt emblazoned with big white letters: "I 'heart' HUMPHREY." Noah could smell a mixture of body odor and syrupy sweetness in the air, the stink you might find in line at the county fair concession stand.

His heart raced; he was nearing a state of pure panic. "Get out of the way!" he screamed as he squeezed through a crush of five more large spectators, all dressed like they were heading to a beach party.

"Hey, dude . . . chill," a skinny teenager with short, blond dreadlocks said as Noah pushed him aside. Noah could almost see the railing. His mind refilled with the soft buzzing sound and he wondered if speedboats were allowed on the river.

Frantic images flashed in Noah's mind. A sunfish leapt from the ocean surface; a mighty whirlpool swirled toward the ocean depths; a mother gray whale swam serenely next to her calf. Trying to shake the pictures from his head, Noah nearly sent a man flying over the railing as he stumbled forward. A deep voice boomed in his mind: "Help us."

The voice was indistinct, like when his mom would yell at Noah from the shower about the list of chores he needed to do. He could never hear her clearly; it was muffled, but he knew what she was saying. Tone. Inflection. Vibrations that made sense deep inside him.

People yelled at him as he made a final push, stuffing himself between two three-year-old kids holding blue toy whales attached to handles that, when squeezed, moved the plastic mouths up and down.

"Look, mister," one of the little boys said as he worked the toy's mouth. He shoved it into Noah's face. "They're talking."

Above the din of the crowd, Noah could hear whale song reverberating from a speaker far below. A microphone immersed in the water caught every nuance. And he could understand what they were saying. At least he thought he could. It was a desperate cry. And he knew he could help . . . if he could just get closer.

He pushed his head tightly against the bars of the bridge railing, straining to see what was going on in the shallows of the murky water. Bright sunlight glinted off the edges of two marine biologists' boats equipped with microphones attached to long booms. The vessels were anchored firmly to avoid being carried away by the river current. Tourist boats circled nearby, filled with sunburnt men and women and their kids snapping pictures to document the ill-fated whales' journey.

He wondered if he was too late; if he should have come earlier. The two whales, a mother and her calf, swam up the river a couple of weeks ago, but Noah hadn't heard anything about it until the news report last night. Now they were stuck. Dying.

Noah had never felt this sense of urgency before. He had never wished for anything harder, urged his mom with such determination. He rarely shouted at anyone, preferring to stay in the background, low key. And he couldn't remember ever shouting at his mom like he did. But instead of screaming back at him this morning and throwing him into his room, she simply grabbed her car keys and dropped them into her purse.

"Fine," she had said, opening the front door and urging him on with a nod of her head, "let's go."

So here they were . . . hundreds of miles away from home. But why? he wondered. What do I do now?

The thrum of vocal intonations returned deep inside his head and Noah struggled to concentrate, trying to figure out what it was saying, to crack the code. The activity around him was too distracting. Suffocating.

"Hey, mister," said one of the kids who was still snapping his plastic whale toy in pantomime. "You want a lick of my lollipop?" The boy held out a large swirled sucker in his other small fist.

A whiff of bubble gum coming off the sticky bulb blasted into Noah's nostrils, making his stomach turn. He started to notice other smells pushed through the sweaty mass of bodies surrounding him: hot dogs, cotton candy, popcorn.

He looked at the crowd with contempt as he used his hoodie to wipe beads of sweat from his brow. He wondered what all these people could be thinking. They were acting like watching whales in distress was some kind of sick amusement park ride. He returned his attention to the water, searching for a sign that the whales were turning back. The large shapes stayed motionless. Somehow he knew what they were feeling: they can't breathe. "Get the boats away from them," he whispered.

Pushing his face hard between the hot steel slats, his cheeks stretching with the strain, Noah could make out the shadow of the dark shapes below—a mother gray whale and her calf languished in the light green river water. A soft puff of spray shot from the larger whale's blowhole. Noah concentrated his thoughts, directing them toward the whales: Go deeper. Back up. Go the other way.

Noah rattled the steel bars, but they wouldn't budge. He felt trapped. The inability to help was overpowering. The mother whale began to head closer to shore. Noah beat his fists against the bars, frantic to make some connection below, but the crowd pushed in, trapping him in a forest of legs and squishing him between the two small onlookers.

"Look! The whale's waving bye-bye," the boy to Noah's left squealed with delight.

"No . . . no," Noah said through the bars, his skull pushing against the hot steel.

A tear rolled down his cheek. Then the noise inside his head stopped. Once again cut off quick, like someone flicked a switch.

Noah knew it was over before the biologists in the boats hung their heads. The mother was dead on the shore. Seconds later, the calf beached itself next to her. Everyone fell silent.

He had failed.

2.

Noah snuck out quietly from his house the next morning, making sure not to wake his mom who was snoring in her bedroom upstairs. He grabbed his bike from the garage, lifting the back wheel so the clacking of the gears didn't sound the alarm. He jumped on and rolled down the dark, deserted Santiempo street toward the beach. He could hear the ocean calling him as he turned into Natural Bridges State Park.

The parking lot was empty. Tendrils of fog still lingered and a light breeze had a damp bite to it, the tang of salt heavy in the air. Noah parked his bike and hiked up a dune to take in the sunrise.

As he looked off in the distance, seagulls hovered above the curling waves that gently pushed the few hard-core surfers, who came out every morning, toward shore. He watched as the waves crashed. Noah knew there were gray whales migrating north this month; he hadn't seen the tiny puffs of spray in the distance since five months earlier.

The expanse of the water looked empty, and he thought of the whales at Klamath—the mother and calf. Tears blurred his vision and he quickly wiped them away with the back of his hand, startled by the sudden rush of emotion. His nose burned as he tried to stuff down his feelings. A tear collected in the webbing between the two lower digits of his index and middle fingers, tracing the pencil thin scar bisecting the skin.

The skin had healed pretty well since he used a razor blade to try and cut the skin that stretched between his fingers, thinking the amateur surgery would fix him. Make him "normal."

His mom found him in the bathroom, his right hand bleeding into the sink as he calmly made the first slice. He nearly took off his finger when she screamed. She rushed Noah to the emergency room, and the doctors fixed it, carefully sewing the skin back together.

He thought it was pretty funny that they took such care to fix an abnormality. His mom's threats of lawsuits probably ensured their precision.

Noah ran a finger slowly along the thin white scar. Thank you so much, you freaking surgeons.

A car pulled up behind him and four boys from his high school began shouting at each other as they started unloading their surfboards. He moved farther away from the group, away from their uncomfortable stares.

Although he had always been a target in the hallways at school, regularly receiving notes and text messages telling him what a freak he was, Noah now thought about the whales and wondered if maybe all those kids were right. Did he really hear them talking to him? Or was he simply losing it?

He moved to the top of the dune and looked across the expanse of ocean near the towering sandstone arches in the water. The natural bridges that had been carved from years of rough seas stood twenty feet from the water's edge.

Three stone arches used to stand stately vigil in the distance, but two had fallen from the force of strong winds and storm surge over the years. Years ago, the public had been allowed to climb the remaining large rock formation, but the park service had stopped that recently to try to keep the last natural structure from tumbling. The thought struck him that Mother Nature might have a different plan.

Noah felt mild electricity in the air. A cool breeze brushed against his face, reminding him of the heavy rainstorm expected later that day. The morning sun shimmered in bars of light on each wave as they broke toward the surface, like the fleeting dashes of Morse code. Noah wondered if the sea was trying to tell him something.

He searched the horizon for any glimpse of a whale spout, wondering if he would hear another call for help—if he would need to send his mom on another seven-hour chase for nothing.

Noah squinted. He swore he could see a dark shape in the water about a hundred yards off shore. The head seemed to bob just inches above the surface of two-foot-high swells.

A strong wind sprayed a fine mist of sea foam from small whitecaps cresting at each peak. As the waves glided in one by one, the small dark head slipped unseen with each rise and fall of the water. He thought it was probably just a sea lion, but it was bigger than what he was used to seeing bobbing in the salty ocean.

Noah made a tent over his eyes. The thing seemed to bob easily, staying hidden.

He tried to pass it off and he pushed away an uneasy feeling. He had almost convinced himself that it was a log, when he saw the thing jump and dive into the water. He was focused on the swells, desperate to find it again, when stinging grains of sand pelted against his face.

Noah scuttled back, ready for a fight.

He looked up to see his friend Taylor Borcelli standing behind him, her long hair cascading over one shoulder in a long ponytail. She was dressed in bright pink running shorts and a Hello Kitty sweatshirt. Unlike Noah, she wore what she liked and didn't care what people said about it.

Being one of the prettiest girls in school helped with her confidence in fashion. She could wear a used plastic garbage bag and still get compliments.

Taylor stood with a fistful of sand held in one hand, the other fist on her hip. "So, you finally crawled out of your hole!"

"Jeez, Taylor! What'd you do that for?"

"You ignore my texts, don't answer my calls? . . . Consider yourself lucky. I thought you were my friend. That's a lousy way to treat me, Noah."

"Sorry, okay?" Noah spit out bits of sand out and shook the grains from his hair. "I was out of town. On a trip."

Taylor plopped herself next to Noah, straight arms resting on her bent legs, rubbing her hands together to dust off the sand. "Still a lousy thing to do," she said with a sideways glance and a sheepish grin.

They sat staring at each other, exchanging silent apologies.

"So, what was the secret trip?"

Noah hesitated.

Taylor turned to Noah, crossed her legs, and placed her chin on her fist. "We've been friends forever. You can tell me anything. So spill it. Where were you?"

"You heard about the wayward whales, right?"

Taylor nodded. "That was so sad. My mom was going to head there; they were asking for more marine biologists to help, but . . ."

"I convinced my mom to drive up to Klamath."

"Did you see them?"

"Yeah," Noah said, grabbing a stick and carving deep grooves in the sand as he spoke. He could feel the burn in his nose, and he willed away the emotion swelling in his chest. The images of the whales on shore flooded his mind. The complete sense of failure pulled him into darkness and he felt as if he was drowning in the sorrow.

"I think I'm going nuts, Tay," Noah whispered.

"Why? Because you wanted to go on a car trip with your mom?"

Noah smiled, his blue eyes sparkling through the nearly spilled tears. "I heard them."

"Heard who?"

"The whales, I think. Or something in my head. It was pushing me there." Noah dug at the sandy hillside, prying out a piece of brush.

"You think the whales were talking to you?"

Noah looked out at the ocean, nodding slightly, unable to look her in the eye. "You don't think I'm a psycho, do you?"

"What, like schizophrenic?"

Noah quickly nodded. "They hear voices, right? Like that."

"I don't think so," Taylor said with a serious, clinical quality. "I looked it up one time after Sophie Jones called me a psycho once in class. Remember her?"

"Not really."

"Anyway," Taylor continued, waving a hand in front of her face, "people with schizophrenia usually hear voices about themselves. Negative stuff. Like they should hurt themselves, or paranoid thoughts, like aliens are communicating to them, directing them, through like the microwave. Is that the type of stuff you were hearing?"

"No. I could barely hear it, really. And it wasn't about me. It was about them. At least I think it was. Like pleading . . . for help."

"Have you ever heard voices in your head before? Is that normal for you?"

Noah was hurt by the question. What is normal for me?

Taylor could tell she struck a nerve, and quickly jumped in. "I'm sorry, Noah. I didn't mean to say it like that. I just meant . . ."

"Yeah, I know," Noah said with a slight grin, still hurt by the word "normal," but trying his best not to show it. He wondered if he would ever get over his insecurity. Noah returned his gaze to the water, hoping for a sign—anything. He willed away the burning in his nose and eyes, the rush in his head as tears threatened to come to the surface. Man up, Noah, he silently chided. He pushed harder to squash the feeling down, anger bubbling up in his desperation to overcome his depression.

"This was the first time for me," he muttered. "I don't remember hearing voices before."

Taylor sat silently staring at him, watching him struggle through his emotions.

Her silence was unnerving. Noah could feel his anger rising inside him, and he searched for a pebble to toss. A big one. Something that could cause some damage. He felt like throwing a ton of rocks into the surf or against the cliffs near the shore. He wanted to feel something, and anger seemed like the easiest way to help him regain some control. He didn't fight it.

"Would you quit staring at me?" he shot at her.

"I—"

"If you want to join up with your friends over there, go ahead."

"Hey, calm down, Noah. I'm just sitting here, okay? Don't put words into my head."

Noah squinted up at Taylor. "Is that supposed to be some kind of a joke? Because I'm hearing crazy whale voices?"

Noah could tell he was making Taylor mad, her brow knit between her soft brown eyes. "I'm sorry," he said, shifting his position, debating whether he should go on. "I'm just freaking out a little bit." He hunched his shoulders, tossing the pebble in resignation; the anger dissipated by the time the stone hit the bottom of the dune.

"So? You do think this is a one-time thing or am I nuts?"

"Give me a minute to process this, okay?"

Noah's heart clenched. He hadn't realized how important Taylor's opinion of him was until now.

"My mom was actually pretty cool about it all," Noah continued quietly. "She didn't ask a lot of questions after we drove all the way up there; she just let me be silent when we drove home." Noah began to toss more pebbles down the slope, mesmerized by the tracks they created as they cascaded down the dune. With Taylor sitting silently, listening, Noah almost felt like he was talking to himself.

Noah could smell a hint of salt in the air, but there was more: a tinge of something rotten coupled with the sweet smell of chocolate from a half-buried Snickers wrapper close by. Noah hated his gift for identifying smells. He noticed and sensed everything around him with a keen awareness. He figured this is how dogs feel when they shove their snouts out car windows. Maybe I'm part dog, he thought.

He looked at the webbing between the lower sections of his fingers, soft skin stretched between the digits from the middle knuckles down to the beginning of his palms. Nope. I'm part something . . . but definitely not dog.

Noah realized he was studying his hands in front of Taylor and quickly shoved them in his pockets. "Anyway, I bet once my mom wakes up, she'll be searching the Internet for some qualified therapists."

An acidic uneasiness bubbled up inside as Noah looked over at Taylor. He hoped what he just told her wouldn't change how she felt about him, hoped he didn't see the same look his mom was giving him last night when they got home.

"I really thought I could do something to help, Tay," he said. "I really thought I was connected to those whales somehow, that they could hear me, understand what was in my head. That if I just got there, I could save them. I've never been so sure of anything in my life, Tay. Maybe I do have a screw loose."

"I've always preferred people with a couple of loose screws." Taylor gave her biggest smile. "Sanity is overrated."

Noah was startled by the dreamy look on her face. Then he laughed; the first hard laugh he had in weeks. "You're crazier than I am."

"Very funny." Taylor grinned. "Anyway, I say you should trust your instincts. And you did. Who knows what we're capable of doing. What our minds can really accomplish. What if you really did hear the whales? Honestly, I think it'd be cool."

"I don't know what it was anymore. At the time, I seemed pretty sure, but now . . . I don't know." Noah ran his hands through his thick hair, his inhibitions retreating for the moment. "It doesn't really matter what it was. I didn't know what to do about it."

Noah watched the surfers ride the gentle waves, the early morning light sparkling on the water with each wave's curl as they thundered onto the sandy beach. His smile began to fade as his mind rekindled the memories of the whales beaching themselves.

Taylor shoved him lightly with her elbow. "Some birthday, huh?"

Noah looked at her, confused.

Taylor smiled, pushing him gently on his shoulder. "It was your birthday yesterday, dummy."

"Oh, yeah."

"How's it feel to be fifteen?"

Noah squinted up at her. "If you asked me that two days ago, I'd have said it was no different."

Taylor smiled at him knowingly. "Hey, let's go into town, grab a bagel, then we can check out the pet shop. That place always cheers you up."

Noah stomach rumbled in agreement. "Looks like the storm's coming in anyway." He took a final look out to sea, the rising waves rolling in majestically.

In the distance, the bobbing creature was back.

Watching.

3.

Taylor and Noah parked their bikes and walked along one of the main Santiempo streets lined with restaurants, coffee shops and used books stores. The streets were crowded for a weekday; smells of rich lattes and freshly baked bread filled the air, as tourists meandered in and out of the shops. Noah was drawn to the smells, realizing he had skipped dinner last night and breakfast this morning. He stopped short near one coffee shop entrance and was almost trampled by a tall long-haired boy in a tie dyed T-shirt and ripped jeans. He was carrying a paper cup with the name Ziggy written on the side.

Taylor grabbed Noah's shirt, pulling him out of the way and steering him into the back of a shorter line at the bagel shop next door. The smells swirled in the small store as they waited, each person carrying a unique aromatic story with them.

Noah always liked to try to connect the smell surrounding someone to a possible backstory. There was a small woman in a green print dress who smelled of coconut and sunscreen.

Obvious tourist, Noah surmised.

A guy with dreadlocks and a stained shirt smelled like skunk.

Stoner.

Noah continued his mental assessments as they waited in line, enjoying each unspoken revelation.

Shoving a warm cinnamon raisin bagel in his mouth as they exited, pedestrians sidestepped around them, shooting furtive glances at Noah's hands as he ate. Noah ignored them; the bagel was the focus of attention. Taylor seemed oblivious to the crowd's reactions to Noah's deformity, something he had always appreciated.

When Noah finished his bagel, he stuffed his hands back deep in his pockets and squashed a smile as he watched Taylor daintily attack her bagel, pushing back her long hair behind one ear before taking a bite. She caught him looking at her, and a flush of blood warmed his cheeks.

Over the past few months, Taylor had grown from a little girl to a young woman, her olive skin nearly flawless, dark lashes encircling the deep brown eyes that now stared at Noah with amusement.

The wind blew papers in looping spirals from the gutters, kicked up a fine dust that made it difficult to breathe, and spit grains of sand into their eyes.

Noah ducked his head away from the blast and pointed to the pet shop across the street. They both ran for the entrance as a strong gust blew a rack of tie-dyed shirts in a spray across the sidewalk.

A bell jingled as they slammed the pet shop door. The walls were a deep blue, and it seemed cooler inside, like they'd stepped into an underwater cave. The air was filled with a cacophony of animal chatter from the stacked cages lining the walls. They were greeted with the caws of caged birds and squeaky wheels turning in mouse cages. But the shop was nearly empty, and aside from the animal noises a loud air conditioning unit was the only other sound.

As they pushed further into the store, a low humming sound whispered in Noah's ear. "You hear that?" he asked.

"What?"

"The buzzing."

"Like bees buzzing?" she asked apprehensively.

"No, it sounds more like static in a speaker." He dug at his ear canal with the tip of his index finger, automatically keeping his other fingers tight to hide his finger's webbing. He rolled his fingers into fists and turned his attention to a gerbil in its wheel.

"Come on," Taylor said, pulling on his sleeve. "You have to see this."

They walked down an aisle filled with fish bowls and colored pebbles, Taylor chatting away about how she thought it was inhumane for people to cage animals and keep fish in tiny bowls just for their amusement, but how the marine lab didn't bother her. "That's the difference between scientific observation and simple barbarianism," she explained.

As they walked, her voice blended with the parrots in a melody of sounds—he let her voice melt into the music of the animal noises as she continued down the aisle, her hair bouncing in rhythm to her chatter.

As he turned the corner near the entrance of the darkened aquarium area, Noah's ears were flooded with a saw blade reverberation. Noah pushed his palms hard against his ears, trying to disengage the sound as he opened and shut his mouth at the entrance, his lips working in a fish-like pantomime.

Taylor paid no attention. "Aren't they beautiful, Noah? Every color you can imagine. And they say most of these fish can be seen out at the Great Barrier Reef." Taylor knelt by a large tank of saltwater fish, running her finger along the glass tracing the path of a brightly colored parrot fish, its beak-like yellow mouth forming small O's as it lazily swam in the water.

"Wouldn't it be great to be able to swim with these guys someday?"

"Yeah, that would be cool," Noah said without inflection, still working his jaw to free the noise filling his head. The buzzing sound was nearly unbearable as Noah stepped farther into the small room. The walls were painted a deep blue, with murals of large exotic fish. The aquarium filters gurgled, but the deafening drone drowned out most of the ambient noise around him. It was almost as if he was hearing a distant radio, the voices incomprehensible among the static, but still recognizable.

Noah peered more closely at the large aquarium sign shaped like a huge tuna that hung above the tanks. He looked for speckled circular holes cut into the colorful wood that might be hiding speakers.

"Come on, Noah. There are a ton of them here!" Taylor called from deeper within the aquatic room, ignoring her friend's unease.

Noah stepped into the dimly lit alcove, and his eyes widened. The garbled, static-filled voices he'd been hearing became more distinct.

He looked at the tanks, the whites of his eyes showing starkly against his pale blue irises.

I must be going crazy, he thought. He could swear the fish were whispering to him.

***

Noah watched Taylor tap against the glass of one of the aquarium tanks, the fish darting back and forth, performing a linear dance. She looked over at Noah, still standing a few feet inside the entrance to the fish area.

"What's wrong? The fish won't bite you," she said. "Check out this one with the long whiskers. This other one's hiding under the rock; you can barely tell it's a fish in there, and this other one, you—"

Taylor rarely took notice of Noah's unique features, but she found herself looking at him in a new way right now. His fingers flexed open and shut. For the first time in a long while, Taylor fell silent. Noah noticed her gaze and quickly shoved his hands into his pockets.

The sound became less garbled as Noah took a step farther into the enclosure. His mouth went slack as he slowly surveyed the different sized tanks flanking the aqua blue walls. As he moved closer to each watered enclosure, the whispering intensified. He looked up at Taylor for any sign she was hearing the same interference from reality.

No connection.

"What's wrong, Noah?" Taylor asked. She leaned in closer to her friend, studying his facial features for signs of epilepsy or stroke. "You okay?"

Noah just nodded, not wanting his voice to interrupt the conversations he was now overhearing. At first, it sounded much like the rinse cycle of a dishwasher—*whish, whish, whish*. But faster . . . much faster.

Noah looked over at Taylor. "You really don't hear that?"

Exasperated, Taylor put her hands on her hips. "Hear what?"

"The voices."

"Is it the same as yesterday? With the whales?"

"It's different. More garbled, and harder to hear," Noah said. He looked at the semi-circle of fish tanks, trying to locate where the whispering was strongest. The fish no longer meandered lazily in the water of the surrounding tanks. They were looking at him. Straight at him. Their bodies lined up like dominoes facing the glass, tails swishing behind them in a synchronized rhythm.

"Look at the fish, Tay," Noah said quietly, his right hand still inside of his pocket, his fingers pushing against the heavy fabric to point at the tanks. "Look."

Taylor walked closer to her friend then noticed the fish. They were all watching Noah, all of them lined the wall of their individual tanks. "That's weird." She looked up at Noah, her grin faltering as she walked along the gurgling tanks, looking intently at each of the different fish: Koi, Puffer, Angel. . . . "What's happening?"

"I wish I knew." Noah knelt down to the floor, his nose just inches from one of the tanks as he stared at a line of fish. The buzzing around him grew louder, and he tried to block it out as he concentrated, trying to decipher the soft garbled whispers.

Something cold and wet hit his cheek.

Then another struck.

"They're jumping!" screamed Taylor.

The tank water seemed to boil as the fish leapt from the water, flopping onto the rubber matted floor.

"Pick them up! Grab them!" she screamed, stumbling around the floor trying desperately to grab the slippery fish. The tops of the tanks were all punched upward and fish were everywhere, the rubber floor mats seeming to vibrate, a shimmer reflecting from tiny scales as their small colorful bodies convulsed, gasping for air. Taylor looked back to see the clerk heading their way.

"What's going on in there?" he called, his heavy boots pounding on the linoleum as he stomped toward them.

Taylor grabbed the sleeve of Noah's shirt, yanking him out the back entrance.

"Run, Noah. Run!"

4.

They stopped when they came to the corner of Front Street and Pacific Avenue, finally catching their breaths long enough to see if anyone was following them. Noah slid down the cool stucco wall of a liquor store, head between his knees as he tried to catch his breath.

Taylor slid down next to him, checking the street to make sure they were in the clear. "I think I might have squished a few of them on the floor when we ran out," she muttered, apprehensively checking the bottom of her shoe for fish goo, hoping she wouldn't find pieces of her favorite fish attached to the rubber sole. "There were so many, I couldn't get around them. And they were so fast. I didn't think fish out of water could move around that fast, but they were everywhere, you know?"

Noah simply nodded, still leaning over his legs with his head down, trying to push away the memory of images that had flooded his mind when the fish were flying around them: scooping nets, large hands reaching toward him, kids with large bulbous eyes and jagged braces sticking out their tongues and making mock fish faces. The images continued to flash in his mind and he pushed his hands hard against his head to try to clear them.

"You okay?" She leaned in close, looking underneath Noah's drooping chin to see his face. "Are you crying?"

Noah looked directly at Taylor, glaring from under his brow. "No."

"I didn't think so, but it's okay if you cry, you know? My dad tells me all the time—" Taylor's voice trailed off.

Noah just blinked at her, trying to cover the uncomfortable silence.

"My dad cries all the time," she continued. "Sad movies, when the Giants won the Series, when I lost my first tooth, when—"

"I wasn't crying, all right?" Noah barked, immediately sorry for how harsh he sounded. He scanned the street once more, and checked his own shoes for fish guts, feeling an intense sorrow for any fish he might have squished when they ran. "What's happening to me?"

He shook his head, tipping it first right, then left. He put his palms against the sides of his head, and removed them quickly like an exaggerated game of peak-a-boo with his ears. The images were gone. The buzzing was gone too. The only noise was from passing cars as they headed toward the beach.

Taylor watched her friend go through the process of clearing his head with a newfound curiosity. Finally, she said, "You really think they were whispering to you?"

Noah hadn't realized she was even listening to him when he said that in the pet shop. He had barely heard it himself. "Yeah," he said. "I think so."

"But you couldn't hear what they were saying?"

Noah leaned against the beige stucco wall, grateful for the shelter from the gusts of wind. "No. It seemed too far away."

Noah closed his eyes and tried to pull the memory up as if opening a file in his brain. "It wasn't like a regular whisper. It was kind of garbled, you know? Like a radio far away on the beach." He didn't know how to mention the flashing images he'd seen in his mind. He was having enough trouble explaining the sounds.

"You think maybe the fish were just too small? You know, like when you have little speakers on a small radio versus those humongous ones they use at the Boardwalk on weekends when they have the fake Beach Boys play concerts?"

"I don't know. Maybe." Noah began moving some of the fine sand on the sidewalk with his toes. "It's like somebody is saying something to me that's really important but it's just out of range, you know? I can feel the intensity of it, but I can't seem to make out the specifics. It's not just a buzzing really. It's more like a crowd of people all talking at once, but really far away. I just can't ever get close enough to know what they're saying. The more I move closer, the farther away the sound gets—just out of reach, you know?"

"And you don't think the sound is people talking, right? You think it's a fish thing?" Taylor asked.

Noah looked up at her through a curtain of his brown hair. "What do you mean?"

"I mean, you think it was just the fish that were whispering to you? I mean, do you think you heard any of the other animals today in the pet shop? The hamsters or the birds? Was it just the fish?"

"I don't know," Noah said with resignation. "I don't think I was hearing the hamsters or the birds. It just happened in the aquarium. And yesterday at the river. It's probably nothing. Maybe an ear infection or something. . . ." He thought about the images he saw in his mind. Or maybe a brain tumor, he thought.

"I just remember hearing a buzz when we came in," he said. "I just thought it was the wind outside or some speaker feedback or something, but then it changed when I saw you with the fish."

"But the fish changed, too," Taylor whispered. "It's like they were standing at attention.   Waiting for commands . . . until they just—" Taylor flung her hands up in the air, mimicking how the fish had reacted.

"Well, I didn't tell them to jump out of their tanks!"

"Maybe you did," Taylor said, looking back up the street at the small pet shop.

"What's that supposed to mean?"

"Nothing," she said, a faraway sound in her voice. "I'm just thinking."

Noah squinted at his friend, waiting. "What are you getting me into now?"

"Just an experiment," she said. "We can do it tonight— at your party at the marine lab. With bigger fish."

5.

Jon Jeffers dropped a three-pronged anchor over the side, letting it sink into the ocean before he sat back on the wooden bench, grabbing his camera, and twisting the lens to bring Natural Bridges and the surrounding beach into clearer focus. Water lapped at the side of his small aluminum boat, as it rocked on the choppy sea. The photographer had draped a large blue plastic rain poncho over his head to keep the fine mist from landing on his camera.

The poncho nearly flew off as a gust of wind pushed at the small craft. "You couldn't wait for a break in the weather?" he chided himself softly as he readjusted the poncho. "Someday I'll get to just take pictures for fun: kids on ponies, butterflies. Retire."

Jeffers was one of the most sought-after wildlife photographers in the area and he never missed a deadline—even when the weather was life threatening.

Two years ago he had been out on a whale watching expedition, trying to get a shot for National Geographic to include in a whale migration spread when a storm came up quickly, nearly capsizing the boat. Although he was pelted with horizontal rain drops the size of gumballs, Jeffers captured some of his best pictures: pitch black skies heavy with rain looming above as two Humpback whales breached from the water.

Jeffers leaned in closer, squatting in the boat's hull, his knees pressed against its sides to keep him from falling overboard. This had better be worth it, he thought. It was the first contract from actual scientists with what seemed like unlimited funding; he saw a lucrative and steady income ahead if he could pull off this assignment.

Although the early-evening sun shone brightly, the wind had stirred up white caps and rocked the boat perilously, pitching him from side to side as he zoomed in on a dark shadow below the surface.

Just one more shot, and I'm out of here, he told himself. He strained harder with his knees, feeling the tension burn through his thighs. Clouds hung low, wisps of grays and whites lining the sky, streaking the last breaths of the recent storm. The camera chattered in quick succession as Jeffers took his last shots of the harbor seals resting on a distant rock.

His legs tingled as they began to fall asleep. He wondered how long he could stand the pain while keeping the camera steady. Just one more shot, he thought. The weight of his body dug against the metal ribbing of the boat interior that held fat bolts securing the wooden seat to the frame. Holding his camera outstretched with his right hand, Jeffers shifted his weight slowly, imagining he looked a lot like his niece at her recent ballet recital. He knew he only had a few more minutes to capture the morning light.

When I get back, I'm asking for a raise, he thought.

A rush of blood slowly returned to his lower extremities and he began to lower himself into a comfortable position, ready to return his camera to its case. "I'll just get back home, download the pictures, crop them and get them to my editor," he said. Since he often worked alone, he was used to keeping himself company. Mainly, he wanted to get back to his house before his Great Dane, Rufus, took a dump on the carpet again.

As he unzipped his canvas case, his weight shifted and he quickly leaned back to adjust for the rocking. A horrible stench filled the air, like the smell of low tide when any rotting fish are exposed on the shore. The boat was recovering when the left side crumpled. Jeffers looked over the side, wondering what he could have hit this far from land. As he reached out toward the crimped metal, the boat was hit again, this time cutting the vessel in half and throwing the startled man into the water.

As the camera sank into the murky depths, the lens captured the reflection of a large mottled gray flipper—and the sharp fangs of the creature as it began to feed.

6.

A Blue whale skeleton held watch in the parking lot, its bleached bones extended alongside the length of one of the green wooden buildings housing the marine life at the Seaside Marine Lab. A large two-story building stood to the left of the skeleton and a slanted metal roof covered large picture windows lining the walls of the discovery center. To the right, a fence ran along the outer edge of buildings housing offices and research facilities as well as the tanks for dolphins, seals and sea lions.

Noah felt a pang of sadness as he looked at the perfectly preserved bones; the skeleton had been there for years, the top of its head standing well above Noah, the body held together with metal fasteners.

"That was a huge find for the lab," a voice whispered from behind him.

Noah turned sharply to see Taylor smiling up at him. "Jeez, Tay. You scared the crap out of me!" he said in a harsh whisper. "Were you raised by ninjas or something?"

"Happy belated birthday, Noah," she said, handing him a small box wrapped in shimmering blue paper. "My mom bought this, and wrapped it before I got home, so it's probably lame."

"Thanks," he said with a lopsided grin. He stuffed the small package into his jacket pocket and surveyed the near-empty parking lot. "Where is your mom, anyway?"

"My dad dropped me off. He had to teach a class tonight at the college, so he might be late, if he can make it. My mom said she still had some work to finish up," Taylor said, rolling her eyes. "You know . . . always working. Where's your mom?"

"She was helping the caterer with the food. Decorating the room; an artist's work is never done. You know. She said to stay away for a bit. She was in single parent overload." He glanced over at where the balloons danced in the wind. "Besides, I was kind of waiting for you."

"Noah?" Taylor asked softly, twirling a long strand of hair around her index finger. "Do you ever miss having a dad?"

Noah looked surprised, but he knew Taylor was only asking out of curiosity. He was more surprised it hadn't come up before—especially considering his birth story. "It's kind of weird to know you came from a test tube," he said with a sardonic grin.

"You're no different from me. My folks went to the same clinic to get help when they wanted to have a kid."

"Yeah, but you know your dad. My mom picked one from a binder."

Taylor pushed him lightly on the shoulder. "Yeah . . . but in the end, she got you."

"Thanks, Tay. That's a pretty nice thing to say." Noah's smile was nearly heartbreaking in its sweetness. Noah could see Taylor's cheeks turn pink under the drape of her ponytail. "To answer your question, no. I don't really miss having a dad. I mean, how can you miss something you never had?"

"Good point." Taylor nodded her chin toward the front entrance. "Come on. Let's get this party started."

***

Tiny pebbles crunched under their feet as the two rushed across the parking lot toward the discovery center.

They could hear glasses clinking as guests sat at their places in a side room designated for parties. Noah was grateful the party was being held away from the aquarium and touch pools. The last thing he needed was another marine mass suicide.

Noah sat next to his mom, who was engrossed in a conversation with another art professor about the early impressionists. He smelled a mixture of hand sanitizer and bleach. Medical technician, he wagered.

Taylor sat on the other side of Noah and her mom sat across from them, smiling pleasantly as she feigned interest in the intricacies of the university art department.

Noah kept his hands in his lap, hoping the menu had stuff he didn't have to use his hands to eat. He quickly scanned the scrolled print on the page. Please, no corn on the cob. No hamburgers. Over the years he'd learned how to hold utensils so they hid his extra folds of skin. Holding onto food, especially something like a giant burger, proved more difficult.

Taylor's mom smiled at Noah as he took a sip of coke. Under her lab coat, she wore a pale green silk blouse that offset her emerald eyes. Strands of her long hair, pulled back in a ponytail, caressed her delicate features, reminding Noah of Taylor in so many ways.

"So, Noah. I hear you had an interesting birthday," Taylor's mom said brightly. "Driving to Klamath? I was so sorry to hear about the whales."

"It wasn't the first time and it won't be the last," Jake Stafford said bluntly before taking a bite of his salad. His dark wavy hair spilled over one eye conspiratorially, the other eye fixed on Noah. "With all the noise pollution in the ocean, the whales are getting lost," he continued. "Finding their way up rivers. Beaching themselves on shore. It's not just trash that's a pollutant, you know."

"Noah," Kate interjected, shooting her companion a warning look, "have you met Dr. Stafford before?"

Noah nodded his head, thinking, "Yes, unfortunately."

"Of course they've met, Kate," Noah's mom added coolly. Jake Stafford had worked at the marine lab with Kate Borcelli since before Noah was born, and much to her chagrin, he basically kept to himself, working diligently behind closed doors.

Taylor always brightened whenever they bumped into him. Noah always found ways to avoid the guy.

He would always creep around in dim hallways staring at the two of them when they were hanging out at the aquarium, and when they started working to help the docents clean up the touch pools. Taylor said it was sweet. Noah felt differently. It got to the point when he could almost sense the guy watching, and would make a game of finding him stuffed away in some dark corner.

For someone so good looking, Jake Stafford seemed to find dark and lonely places to hang out.

"Nice to see you again, son," Jake said without inflection, looking unblinkingly at Noah.

"Yeah," Noah replied with indifference.

"Shake hands with Doctor Stafford," Noah's mom mumbled through a bite of salad, pointing her fork in Jake's direction.

Noah hesitated, his hands clenched tightly in his lap. Why did she always push hand shaking? She left his hands like this. She saw what he tried to do two years ago—and then fixed it! But she was always telling him to shake people's hands, telling him how it was a sign of respect. And every time Noah would comply, he could almost feel the shiver of revulsion being transferred from one hand to another.

His mom glared at him as seconds ticked silently away. He wiped off his sweaty palms and extended his right hand, giving Dr. Stafford's a quick shake. Noah saw the flicker of eye movement to his fingers, the light touch of skin on skin, and the stiffness of Stafford's facial muscles before a fake smile bloomed across his perfect lips, unveiling his gleaming white teeth.

Noah's heartbeat marked off the uncomfortable milliseconds of contact before Taylor chimed in to all the guests at the table: "Did you know Dr. Stafford is an expert on water pollutants? His research is focusing on climate change and its effects on marine life."

Stafford quickly pulled his hand back and shot Taylor his dazzling smile, all dimples. "Why thank you, Taylor. I had no idea you were such a fan of my work."

"Our work," Taylor's mom corrected curtly before taking a bite of lettuce.

"I saw you on TV when you were protesting at the college," Taylor said with a smile, ignoring her mother. Noah could almost feel the heat radiating from her blushing cheeks. Although he was grateful that the focus had shifted away from him, he was getting really tired of hearing about the brilliant Dr. Jake Stafford. "I think what you and my mom are doing is so important."

"Oh, yeah?" Jake shot Kate a sideways glance.

"What did you hope to do up there with the whales?" Kate said with a little too much enthusiasm.

Noah shrugged, trying to look nonchalant. "I just wanted to see them."

"Your mom said you were a bit . . . frantic," Kate pushed on.

Noah's mom had returned to her chat about impressionists with the man sitting next to her in a loud tie-dyed T-shirt. Noah's eyes bored holes into the back of his mom's head as it bobbed in animated conversation, oblivious to his embarrassment.

He looked back at Taylor's mom, feeling beaten, as if everyone—except his mother—was watching him. "I just had a feeling they weren't going to make it, Dr. Borcelli. I thought if I could get up there . . ."

Stafford, staring intently at Noah, rested his chin on his hands pressed together in a steeple. "What?" he asked sharply. "If you got up there . . . you thought what?" His tone was similar to one you would use with a small child who had just been caught with his hand in a cookie jar.

Noah looked at Taylor, silently pleading with her to change the subject again, but she was no help. She was too busy staring dreamily at Dr. Stafford, who was oblivious to her gaze. The depression from that morning on the beach flooded back in. "I just thought I could help," he croaked.

"Why would you think that?" An uncomfortable silence fell over the table and more seconds passed. The only sound was his mom's giggle, which ended abruptly when she realized no one was talking.

Finally, the medical technician broke the tension.

"You surf, don't you Noah?" she asked.

Noah opened his mouth to respond when his mom chimed in, a light lilt in her voice: "Noah hasn't been in the ocean—or even the deep end of a pool since he was six."

Noah dropped his chin to his chest, his dark hair falling in an embarrassed drape across his face. Perfect. *Now* she joins the conversation.

"You don't swim?" Jake asked, his eyebrows arched in a question. "And you live in a beach town?"

"It's my fault, really," Noah's mom answered for him with another giggle. "He tried to swim once, but it was a miserable failure. When he was six, I took him to that community pool over by Schlotzky's Big and Tall that all the kindergartners went to—you know the one – "

"The one that smells like chlorinated urine," Noah mumbled into his salad.

"Noah!" his mom said, feigning shock.

"I wanted to 'expand his horizons,' teach him a new skill," she continued lightly. "Honestly, I didn't think it would be that hard . . ."

"If I remember right, I think you just liked one of the swim coaches," Noah said with a sideways glance. "Single mothers always seem to have potential boyfriends in the back of their minds when they're planning outings," he explained, staring directly at Stafford as he spoke.

"Noah!" his mom cried. "Really!"

"Come on, Mom," Noah said with utmost seriousness. "You have to admit we went to a lot of firehouses when I was a kid. I knew what you were doing when you had me take that first aid and CPR class last year. You were all over the fire chief."

The group gathered at the table sat in shocked silence. Taylor's fork hung in mid-air near her open mouth, eyes glued on Noah's mom, waiting for a reply.

Seconds ticked away. Then Noah's mom smiled brilliantly. "You know . . . he's right," she said to the group. "That fire chief was gorgeous." Polite laughter skittered around the room before she continued.

"Anyway . . . Noah decided to go in the deep end at the pool. You had one of those foam floating boards, remember Noah?" She didn't wait for an answer. "Well, next thing I know, Noah's at the bottom of the pool, near the drain, looking up at the kids playing and swimming past him."

Noah remembered that day. As he went deeper, his extremities started to tingle and his chest felt tight, but it wasn't a bad thing. It felt like when your hands or feet fall asleep, kind of heavy and a pins and needles thing. His eyes hurt, too, at first, but then he could swear he could see people distinctly at the far side of the pool, in the shallow end.

"He was just sitting down there, his legs crossed and his arms pushing up against the water to keep submerged, watching big bubbles come out of his mouth."

"What did you do, Cheryl?" Kate asked.

"Yeah, Mom," Noah chuckled, giving his mom a knowing sideways glance. "Tell them. What did you do?"

"I did what any self-respecting mother would do," she said defiantly. "I jumped into the pool."

"Fully clothed," Noah added with a sad grin.

"No way," Taylor said, eyes wide.

Noah shrugged his shoulders, shaking his head slowly, reliving the memory. "She nearly drowned me trying to save me. The swimming instructor had to pull us both out of the water," he said, "so that love affair never materialized."

Then, returning to look at Stafford, he added, "And so I never learned how to swim."

"Well, you could have, Noah. I just—"

"Really, Mom?"

"So," Taylor blurted to her mom, desperate to change the subject, "what time do we have to be at the beach tomorrow?"

"We'll start early," she said. "Noah and Taylor volunteered to clean up the beaches with us tomorrow, Jake. Isn't that nice? Noah's always been one of our biggest helpers around the aquarium and touch pools. Always willing to pitch in when they need something done. Isn't that right, Noah?"

"I help, too," Taylor interjected.

Kate glanced at her daughter, smiling. "Of course you do, Taylor." She took a bite of salad and continued to list off the times Noah had helped around the center. "And Noah is a veritable encyclopedia of knowledge about anything involving marine life," she continued. "You're going to be a docent this year, right?"

"Taylor always seems to know more than I do," Noah said as he gave an encouraging smile to his friend.

"Oh, I don't think that's true, Noah," Kate countered, oblivious to how her comments were affecting Taylor, who sat in stunned silence, her face ashen. "Remember when we were having that issue with algae blooms, and you figured out the solution without much thought at all?" She turned to Stafford. "It really was amazing, Jake," she added. "Do you remember me telling you about that?"

"No. Seems you haven't told me everything about our birthday boy." Stafford watched Noah intently, staring at the teen's hands as Noah placed his glass back on the table. An uneasy feeling crept up the back of Noah's spine and he slid his hands back into his lap as Taylor's mom continued to dump praise his way.

"Mom, I think you're embarrassing Noah," Taylor said. "Maybe we could change the subject."

"I'm sorry, Noah. I just think you're amazing and everyone should know that on his birthday. Don't you agree, Jake?" She looked at Stafford encouragingly and waited for his reply.

"Sure," he said flatly, before offering a sardonic grin. "Happy birthday, kid."

Noah leaned over to Taylor and through a fake toothy grin, whispered, "Get me out of here."

7.

The wind had died down by the time Noah and Taylor escaped and began to walk along the bluffs. Pewter clouds hung heavy in the distance, outlined by the light of a full moon. The moonlight shimmered off of Taylor's long brown hair, making her skin seem almost luminescent. Noah considered holding her hand, but the thought of her fingers caressing the excess skin between his made him stuff his fists deeper into his pockets. He sidestepped around a clump of lavender on the path, regaining his composure.

"What is with that guy?" Noah asked. "He always stares at me like I'm in some kind of specimen jar."

"You mean Doc Stafford?"

"Yeah, your dreamy doctor," Noah said sarcastically. "Doc Adonis. Doctor Strange."

"Nothing's wrong with him. He's a really cool guy, actually; you just have to get to know him. And he's super smart. I'm learning a lot about the environment from him and about his work. And he's really nice. Whenever my mom is stuck in a meeting or working on her research, he talks to me when I'm waiting in their office. He's doing things that will benefit humanity, Noah."

"Jesus. You sound like you have a real crush on the guy." Noah shook the tangles of brown hair away from his eyes with mild irritation.

"Don't be stupid."

"No, seriously, Tay," Noah said, mimicking her in a singsong voice. *"He's so smart, so funny, and I learn so much.* I saw how you were around him tonight; all excited like a puppy. But the guy's more than twice your age. What is he, like thirty?"

"Thirty-nine."

"That's a little embarrassing, don't you think?"

"Maybe my intellect requires a more mature companion," Taylor huffed.

"You're kidding, right? You're fifteen."

"I'll be sixteen in six months."

"There are laws against that, you know."

Taylor looked back at the discovery center, the interior brightly lit and the adults chatting amicably at the table, Dr. Stafford among them. Noah caught her dreamy look.

"What do you like about that guy anyway? Does he even have a doctorate?"

"He got his Ph.D. in genetics from U.C. Davis, if you must know. And a bachelor's in biology. He's super smart."

"Yeah, I heard you the first hundred times," Noah said with an eye roll. "If he's so smart, how come he's just your mom's assistant?"

"He's not really her assistant as much as a co-worker. He was brought on board to help her with this special project they've been working on for years. Really hush-hush stuff. Anyway, I'm surprised you never heard of him before." Taylor sat on a cement bench overlooking the bluffs. The waves crashed against the cliffs below. "He was on the environmental task force with the city and the university to stop dumping in the oceans, and he worked with the city of Santiempo to enact the most stringent recycling laws in the state."

"Okay, so he loves the planet. But what is it, really? His long wavy hair? His dimples when he smiles? His big muscular arms?"

Taylor turned to face Noah, arms across her chest. "Now you sound like you have a crush on him."

Noah snorted at that.

"Let's not talk about him any more."

"Fine by me."

Taylor looked back at the yellow light shining through the large windows of the discovery center, the sound of adult laughter floating toward them over the dry brush on the hillside. "I wanted to come out here while all the adults are in there talking; they should be busy for a while. This might be a good time to do some real digging." She gave a wicked grin and held up her small digital recorder, the size of a small candy bar. "I've been thinking about the fish this morning and your . . . um, voices . . . and thought we could use this to try to pick up on frequencies too low for the human ear to hear. I saw these investigators use it on a ghost hunting show one time. What do you think?"

Noah gave a noncommittal nod and shrugged his shoulders.

"Then come on."

They walked back up the path toward the buildings behind the parking lot and stopped at a large fence emblazoned with the words No Trespassing and Authorized Personnel Only. A strong wind blew through the bleached whale skeleton, causing an eerie whistling sound, like a far-off high-pitched scream, a warning from beyond.

"You think it's okay to go in there?" Noah asked, the thought of getting caught needling in his brain.

"Sure," Taylor said, with a wistful smile. "This is going to be fun."

***

The side gate hinges squeaked in protest as Taylor pushed it open.

"This way," she said.

Cool air greeted them as they entered the hallway past a heavy metal door. Water gurgled through an intricate web of overhead pipes that fed the tanks housing the onsite marine life, reminding Noah of the aquarium earlier that day.

It felt like years since they watched the fish fly from their tanks. He felt a pang of remorse, thinking of the fish that had jumped, and wondered if the owners of the store were able to save any of them.

His footfalls were muffled by the floor's rubber matting, Noah followed Taylor in a series of turns, wondering if he should be dropping breadcrumbs on the ground as they pushed on through the maze of hallways.

They finally stopped in front of a large metal door; the large deadbolt and sign stating Authorized Personnel were no deterrent for Taylor, who searched her pocket for a key to get in. Noah caught a musty odor that seemed to slither up from the crack between the door and the floor.

When Taylor opened the heavy door, the smell slammed into Noah and he stifled a cry, pinching his nose closed with his hand.

"What's wrong?" Taylor hissed.

"You don't smell that?" Noah mumbled through his plugged nose.

Taylor shook her head, then scanned right and left before pulling Noah inside. The door clicked shut with finality behind them. She continued walking, turning down another corridor.

"Just around here," she whispered.

Noah breathed through his mouth, trying his best to push down the smell. The buzzing sound began to fill his head as they made the last turn. He immediately regretted his decision. The room was dark, a soft blue light reflecting off the water, creating a kaleidoscope of shimmering movement on the ceiling.

"How do you know your way around this part of the lab so well?" Noah whispered. "I thought it was a secure area."

Taylor just smiled with a shrug. "You know me."

"Yeah," Noah said, rolling his eyes.

"Do you hear any voices?"

"No. No voices." But Noah knew something was happening.

"I want to show you something." Taylor's voice echoed softly off of the cement walls. "A seal that was born here. My mom's been working with it on some communication techniques—kind of like Morse code. She can get them to do stuff for her by tapping and sliding on the outside of the tank with these."

Taylor grabbed a small wooden oar that was leaning between two pipes. Taylor tucked a long strand of hair behind her ear as she walked next to Noah, swinging the oar casually, but careful not to hit the walls.

"I can call it over. See if anything happens inside you . . . like at the aquarium." She tapped the oar lightly on the side of her head for emphasis, then leaned over and began to slide the oar against the side of the tank.

"Did you ever hear of the psychology professor in Honolulu who did a bunch of experiments with bottle-nose dolphins, teaching them to interact?" she asked. Tap. Slide. "It was back in the 1970s, this guy Louis Herman was trying to see if he could teach his dolphins to communicate with humans. He worked with the dolphins for about twenty years and they learned more than thirty signals, including nouns and verbs. My mom couldn't stop talking about him for a while. He could tell the dolphins to get things using signals, and he could mix the signals to tell the dolphins to do things like get a surfboard, or bring a man to a surfboard. Stuff like that. It was really a breakthrough experiment.

"Don't get me wrong . . . the guy was kind of weird," she added. Tap. Slide. "He lived with the dolphins, like a hermit in a cave with an assistant, and I think there were some strange accusations about him. It was a long time ago." She brushed away the thought with her hand. "But it was ground-breaking work at the time. Anyway, my mom was obsessed with the guy. Wanted to follow in his footsteps, I guess.

"She's been working on this program, expanding on his research, trying to communicate with marine life," she said as they took another turn. "She thinks it would allow us to work together as the planet evolves . . . you know with climate change, and stuff."

Taylor looked over at Noah, her smile faltering when she saw him swaying. "You okay, Noah?" Taylor asked, concerned. "You're not looking so good. Should we go back?"

"I'm okay," he said, pinching the skin between his brow.

"You sure? You don't look right."

The salty smell in the air had an undertone of something rotting just under the surface. He wondered if the area was too damp; if mold had accumulated under the floor mats.

Strange images began to flash in his mind—fangs snapping in strong jaws, close-ups of ruined flesh, torn and bleeding. The humming sound intensified as he moved closer to the tank.

"Are the voices back? Should I turn on the recorder?"

"It's—yeah, maybe." He shook his head, trying to flush the images from his mind. "Can I sit down somewhere?" he asked, weakly. "I think I'm going to puke."

"Oh, crap. Yeah . . . um, over here."

Noah sat on a metal bench propped against a concrete wall, but it only made things worse. "I think I need some fresh air," he said weakly.

"Sure, let's get you out of here." Taylor grabbed his arm and helped prop him up, concern washing over her face.

A high-pitched scream began building in Noah's mind as they turned to go. He turned to look behind him at the dark area that housed the partially sunken water tank; it was twenty feet wide and eight feet deep, with a three-foot ridge around its perimeter.

At first Noah thought he could see the seal in the tank, bobbing near the surface. Then he saw its mottled flesh, its red bulbous eyes. As the creature ducked underwater, the full force of the scream ripped through Noah's mind.

Taylor held on to him as she pushed through the large metal door, slamming it shut behind them. The scream stayed with him, though. Noah began to wonder if he was hearing the scream in his mind, or if he was the one screaming.

8.

The large round clock above the heavy door slowly ticked off the seconds as Noah and Taylor slid quietly into her mom's office. Noah took a seat on a black leather swivel chair and dropped his head into his hands.

"What's happening to me?" he asked, trying to will away the memory of the scream that had followed him down the darkened hallways.

"Are you feeling better?" Taylor asked, one hand precariously touching Noah's shoulder.

Noah looked up through his drooping hair, cleared his throat, and tried to get back to a sense of normalcy.

"Yeah . . . aside from voices and screams echoing around in my head on a regular basis, I'm just great."

"Maybe we got something on this." She began to play back the digital recording.

"Nothing," she said. Disappointment creased her brow as she tucked the recorder back in her pocket.

Taylor scanned the office, noting the specimen jars on the shelves and the paperwork neatly stacked on gleaming metal tabletops. She stood up and placed the small oar she had been carrying since they left the tanks against a metal file cabinet.

Reaching into her backpack, she pulled out a key ring and started sifting through the large assortment of keys. Finding a small gold key, she unlocked the top cabinet, and began sifting through its contents.

Noah watched in horror. "Are you nuts?"

Taylor grabbed a bright green folder and sat on the bench next to Noah, flipping through pages of notes and charts.

"What are you doing?" Noah asked in a harsh whisper. "We shouldn't be in here messing with stuff."

"I'm not messing with anything," Taylor said, emphatically. "I'm reading."

She flipped through a few more pages, quickly scanning them with her index finger. "This is the data about my mom's project—the one I was telling you about. The communication project with the marine mammals here at the lab. But this doesn't make any sense."

"Why not?"

She opened the top drawer of the file cabinet and began searching again. She pulled out a dark red file marked Notes, the pages filled with her mother's tiny immaculate cursive.

"The data she was collecting is really weird. And check this out." Each stapled group of papers had a photo attached to the outside corner. "Most of these seemed to be some type of seal or sea lion." Taylor felt like she was looking through mug shots, files of the woeful specimens that had died at the lab.

The office was deathly quiet. The only sound in the lab was the drip from a leaking faucet and the soft rustle of pages as she read. Noah listened for any footsteps in the hallway, but the hum of the water filters masked any sound from outside.

Taylor clicked on a desk light, illuminating a metal table as she began to flip through more pages in the folder. She stopped at a page filled with a colorful map of the coastline.

The folder also contained an article about how methylmercury had been found in larger quantities of tuna and cod pulled from waters off the California coast near Marker 6, five miles southwest of Lighthouse Field State Beach. Maps with tiny colorful dots filled the page and arrows pointed to several locations where concentrations of contaminated fish were found.

"Would you put that stuff away? Somebody could walk in here any second!" Noah kept his eyes on the small window at the center of the door, looking for any shadow in the hallway to alert him of people coming.

Taylor continued to flip through pages, ignoring him, showing no concern of being interrupted. "Do you remember anything about a spill near here?"

"What kind of spill?" The clock seemed louder now, counting down to their impending doom.

"Toxins. Or any kind of illegal dumping in the area. The concentration of dots on the map look like a semi-circle . . . around Natural Bridges."

"I know people on the news have been talking about how the ocean is getting more polluted. About that giant island of garbage floating around in the Pacific. It was due to some kind of fishing net, right?"

"Yeah, I remember hearing about that," Taylor said as she flipped to another page. "But this data seems to be more about chemicals."

Noah took another furtive glance at the closed door.

"My mom and Doc Stafford were talking one time about synthetic chemicals and their effects on wildlife," Taylor continued, oblivious to Noah's unease. "They said one of the reasons that this kind of stuff is so potent is due to the tendency to reach progressively higher concentrations with increasing levels in the food web; they called it biomagnification. They were pretty upset about it, but that was years ago. Look!" she said, holding up an article clipping. "This is about plastic debris churning into a sludge that hangs in a heavy, lumpy film across the Gulf of Mexico. Like you were talking about."

"You should put that stuff away," Noah cautioned. "We could get caught and get ourselves—"

"And this article is about the hypodermic needles that washed ashore on Long Island beaches. Remember that? And this one . . . whoa!" She silently read, her dainty finger running along the text on the page. "Did you know children in India dig through discarded appliances, searching for mercury, copper, and other metals?" She flipped through a couple more pages.

Noah was amazed at the speed she could read.

"But what does this have to do with her project?" Taylor asked herself. "What does this have to do with finding a way to communicate with marine mammals?"

"Taylor, put . . . it . . . away."

"I just want to check one thing." She returned the file, closed the top drawer softly, and rolled a chair over to the computer. She entered the password her mom used at home. Noah secured the deadbolt on the door and once again looked out the small rectangular window to make sure no one was coming.

All clear.

The office echoed with a loud beep from an error message that popped up when Taylor typed in the last letter.

"She changed her password," she whispered to herself.

Taylor began to look behind the monitor and under the keyboard, then began running her fingers underneath the countertop.

"Now what are you doing?" Noah whispered harshly.

"It's a common place people hide their passwords. They had a story about it recently. People are always forgetting the new ones and—hey! I found it!" She pulled out a Post-it note from under the counter and immediately began typing in numbers. "See?"

Noah felt light-headed, the tension pulsating through his throat, but Taylor paid no attention. She was already typing. Another error alarm sounded off and words of warning filled the screen.

"Dang. The password isn't numeric."

"Maybe it's in code," Noah said without thinking, eyes still glued on the door.

Taylor's eyes widened in excitement. "Yeah. Like that alphabet game we used to play. Each number corresponds to the letter in the alphabet. A is one, B is two . . ." Taylor handed Noah the Post-it note and swiveled back to the computer. "Read me the numbers, and I'll type them in."

Noah slowly said the numbers, taking time to check the door as he read: twenty . . . eighteen . . . nine . . . four . . . five . . . fourteen . . . twenty.

"T . . . R . . . I," Taylor said as she slowly typed in the letters corresponding with the numbers Noah read, "D . . . E . . . N . . . T."

Trident.

***

The adults from the party had flooded into the lobby area next to the aquarium and were busily chatting and sipping their drinks. The din of the festivities echoed off the high ceiling, and Jake pushed through the guests, looking for Kate. He finally found her in a dark corner in a heated discussion about the evils of soft plastic.

He sidled up to the group and touched her arm, leaning in to whisper in her ear. "We have a problem."

Kate smiled politely, and excused herself before walking off with Jake.

"What's going on?" she asked.

"Your daughter and the birthday boy are nowhere to be found."

"They're fine. It's Noah's birthday. They're probably looking at the jellyfish."

"I checked there. They're not anywhere outside either."

"What are you so worried about?"

"You sure they couldn't get into the tank area?"

"Why would they do that?"

"This isn't the first time Taylor—"

"If she went in there, I'll take care of it," Kate said, putting her glass on a cocktail table and turning to go. "It's my responsibility, Jake."

"No offense, Kate, but this is a little too important to put Taylor on restriction or take her phone away. If she compromises our—"

"I get it," Kate said sharply. "Let's go find them; then you can stop worrying."

"Stop worrying about what?" Noah's mom asked brightly from behind them.

9.

The sound of soft clacking of the keyboard filled the lab office, each strike sending shockwaves of dread down Noah's spine. And it seemed to get louder with each passing second.

Noah's mind began to wander back to the fish lined up in their tanks—and the thing he had seen tonight floating near the surface of the tank down the darkened hallway behind the locked door. Why was this happening? He wondered how often teenagers go nuts.

The computer erupted with another loud beep. Noah felt like he was going to hurl. Clandestine work wasn't his strong suit; he always sat at the front of the class, followed directions, and never talked back to adults. Breaking into someone's computer was definitely out of his comfort zone. But deep down inside, he admitted he liked the thrill.

He looked over at Taylor with admiration. She never flinched when it came to stressful situations. Noah, on the other hand, frequently freaked out.

When they were around eight years old, Taylor convinced him to break into an old abandoned house at the end of a dark street downtown. It had been boarded up for years and every Halloween kids at their elementary school would start to spread rumors about the murders that took place there, and how the place was haunted. It was like showing a dog a nice juicy bone. Taylor brought a candle and matches—strictly forbidden in Noah's house—and planned to do a séance once they got inside.

Noah remembered how beautiful Taylor looked, even as a little girl, when she lit that candle. And he remembered how when she asked the candle a question, the flame flickered, sending Noah running. He shot out so quickly he never saw the police cruiser pulling up. A neighbor had spotted the two of them prying off the weathered piece of plywood on the side door and called the cops. Taylor was taken home and promptly put on restriction, and Noah slid away without any repercussions. But it was Noah who became more wary after that. Taylor just kept plugging along, looking for trouble.

"We're gonna get caught, Taylor," he whispered. "I just know it."

"Calm down, Noah," Taylor responded quietly, her gaze intent on opening the window on the screen.

His gaze shifted between the illuminated computer screen to the locked door just a few feet away. He swore he heard footsteps outside. A trickle of sweat rolled down the back of his neck.

"Come on, we have to get off the computer."

"I know, Noah. I'm almost there."

The screen flashed with green letters: Trident Initiative.

"How did you do that?"

Ignoring him, Taylor clicked on a data file and a chart filled with alphabetized names, dates, and times. She immediately recognized the first name: Alpha. "These are the same names as the seals in the paper file from the cabinet," she said. "But this is more detailed. And it seems to be linked to something else."

"I swear I hear someone coming," Noah whispered. A new bead of sweat formed on Noah's temple.

Taylor continued to scroll down through the data on the screen. "Have you ever heard of this?"

"I've heard of Trident, the gum. And the thing the Little Mermaid's dad used that the octopus lady wanted so badly."

Taylor gave Noah a sideways glance. "We can talk later about your princess movie knowledge."

Noah checked the lock again. "Just get off the computer before someone comes, okay? We're going to get in a ton of trouble."

"I need to print this," Taylor said calmly.

The printer sounded like a buzz saw in the quiet lab room. "Watch the door, okay?"

"What do you think I've been doing?" Noah willed the printer to finish, go faster. It droned on, slowly spitting out the pages.

His heart racing, Noah peered out of the small rectangular window in the center of the upper portion.

"Someone's coming!" he hissed.

Taylor closed out the window on the computer, quickly shut off the monitor and grabbed the sheets of paper from the printer. She tucked the pages into her pocket just as the door clicked open and her mom stepped through the door.

***

The silence was palpable as Kate stared at her daughter, her slender right index finger ticking away the seconds against her folded forearms. Jake stood slightly behind her, letting her take the lead, but obviously perturbed. Noah thought he seemed almost exultant. Noah's mom peaked from behind the man's broad shoulders.

Kate Borcelli let out a heavy sigh. "I'm really not sure what to say, Taylor. You know my office is off limits." She shifted her gaze to Noah, the disappointment creased in her brow, reminiscent of Taylor's look earlier. "And to bring Noah into this. On his birthday."

Taylor looked at the adults gathered around them. "We weren't snooping, Mom. Really. We were trying to—"

"—see the dolphins," Noah interrupted. He looked over at Taylor as he quickly continued. "I asked Taylor to take me. It's my fault. When we got close, I started to feel sick—probably too much cake or something. We were trying to find our way back and we got lost."

Jake chimed in, "I don't mean to be a jerk, but I'm pretty sure I saw you guys leaving the restricted area. You've been around here long enough to know that's off limits."

"Taylor?" her mom asked. "Is that true? Were you in the restricted area?"

"I was so worried about Noah, I didn't realize we were over there," Taylor said, applying one of her most innocent of looks. "I'm sorry."

Noah's mom clapped her hands together loudly behind Jake, startling everyone.

"Well, great. Just a big misunderstanding!" she said with gusto. "If we're all finished here, we should get back to the party."

"Of course," Taylor's mom opened the door to let them out. "I'm sorry we pulled you away, Cheryl," she added, taking her friend's arm. "Lock up behind us, okay Dr. Stafford?"

Jake nodded, trying to stuff down his irritation at being treated like an underling. He watched them all file out of the office and head down the hall, Cheryl's bubbling voice a soft echo as she chatted with Kate.

As he switched off the lights and pulled the door shut, securing the deadbolt, he noticed a blinking light through the door's small rectangular window.

He reopened the door and entered the darkened room. In the corner, the printer was on. An error message pulsed on the small LED screen: load paper.

Jake grabbed a stack of paper from a nearby drawer and inserted it into the tray. The printer roared to life, printing the final page outlining the Trident Initiative.

10.

The last thing Noah wanted to do the next day was to go near water, but he promised to help clean up the beach and after last night, and he didn't want to let Taylor or her mom down.

"Hey, you're early," Taylor called, running up to greet him. She held long sticks with serrated ends and two canvas trash bags that they could sling over their shoulders as they collected trash. She handed one to Noah. "You doing okay today?"

"Yeah, all good," Noah lied. The buzzing sound had returned as soon as his mom turned into the parking lot. He didn't want to bring it up. He was sick of the whole thing and hoped it would just go away.

That's what happened when you had a cold, right? You feel like crap, then things work themselves out.

Taylor looked down the beach to see where her mom was standing. "I need to tell you about what we printed last night," she whispered. "But talking about it here isn't the best idea."

Noah's head ached, so he was happy to skip talking about anything right then.

He pointed to a clump of scrub in the distance. "I think I'll head over there to start. Meet up with you later?" he asked.

"Sure." Taylor smiled and held the poker up in a mock salute. "I'll catch up with you later. Happy hunting." She turned away, meandering up a dune in search of trash.

The poker was slick. The long pole slipped through Noah's fingers as he tried to stab at the debris stuck under small drifts of sand. A bit farther down the beach, a group of cheerleaders and football players from his high school were combing through the brush and laughing.

He looked off into the distance. Seagulls hovered above the dark gray waves that gently curled forward, holding deeply tanned surfers aloft before crashing into the Santiempo shoreline. He was glad to be away from the others, away from their uncomfortable stares.

He tried to focus on piercing the trash stuck deep under large tangles of seaweed, but he felt exposed. Each jab had the potential of a clumsy miss. He stepped further away from the group. Their laughter called out behind him through the whistling wind as it tossed his dark brown hair wildly around his head.

The clouds grew heavy; a dark gray curtain of rain fell in the distance. Noah wound around the dusky dunes, searching for glints of color or shimmers of aluminum to grab, doing his best to stay focused.

He jabbed at a crumpled Reese's wrapper and stuck it in the canvas sack, marveling at how people could just toss their garbage on the ground as if it would just disintegrate like magic. As he climbed up a small mound of sand, a blanket of tiny flies lifted lazily in the air like a black shroud before dropping lightly down to feed on the artificially sweetened sandy surface near a crumpled Coke can.

He stabbed at a soggy candy wrapper, but the pole was slick and shot free nearly hitting his chin. He checked behind him to see if anyone saw the miss. The other kids were just dots in the distance. Separate.

Noah pushed his hair aside before tightening his grip around the pole, taking aim at an empty coffee cup. He pierced the Styrofoam, punching more holes as he mumbled to himself.

"This is for you, you frigging litterbugs," he said, enunciating each word as he stabbed perfect holes in the soft cup.

Taylor came up from behind him, looking over his shoulder. He jumped when she spoke. "Jeez, Noah. Calm it down a notch. You'd think you were some kind of Nordic hunter or something." She gave him a sideways grin, shifting her gaze to the cup.

"I think it's dead," she said, kicking it softly.

Noah jabbed meekly at the tattered cup. "I guess I got a little carried away."

"Teresa Munroe just told me my mom found a necklace with her metal detector that's pretty cool," Taylor said as she pointed at her mom, who was slowly dragging a metal disc attached to a long stick across the sandy beach. "But let's steer clear of her right now. I've been avoiding her all morning. I'm on the verge of being grounded for a month. And it would have been longer if your mom didn't get us out of that mess last night. I owe her one." She pointed to a dune closer to the ocean. "You want to try over there?"

The beach was right across the pier from the Santiempo Boardwalk, sitting inside a small cove that butted against cliffs extending along West Cliff Drive. Hotels dotted the roadside before the winding pavement meandered higher where regal homes had stood watch over the ocean since the 1920s.

Taylor kicked up tiny swirls of sand as she ran over the dune, a strong gust of wind catching it and blowing it out to sea. A blast of fine grains flew into Noah's mouth. His teeth crunched with the grit, the tang of salt on his lips. Off in the distance, waves crashed on shore pushing foamy lace curtains of water onto the wet sand. The shallow water rushed swiftly past a large black lump covered in a film of sand and tangled seaweed.

As Noah got closer, he thought it might be an old couch cushion or discarded duffle bag that had washed ashore. Maybe it's filled with cash, he thought, fantacizing about escaping to a small island where servants would wait on him hand and foot—no uncomfortable stares, no awkward silences. Then the wind shifted and the smell hit him—a mixture of rotting eggs and soggy wet spinach—the kind his mom would force on him every Sunday night for dinner.

He stopped short, watching Taylor backpedaling just a few feet in front of him.

She covered her mouth, her face a tight grimace. "God! What is it?" She started to take a step closer, turning her head away from the smell as she walked. It definitely was not a person. The surface of the large brown lump shifted like a mirage as a blanket of biting flies rose and settled again to feed.

Noah grabbed Taylor before she could go any further to investigate. "Taylor, wait! You don't know what that thing is."

"Nothing that smells that bad can be alive," she mumbled from under her hand.

"Just wait. We don't even know if it's dead." Noah inched forward, the garbage pick held above his shoulder like a warrior's spear.

Taylor was now only about a foot away from the sandy mass, pinching her nose hard and squinting her eyes as her long brown hair whipped in frenzied arcs around her head.

Noah held his breath as he inched closer. The lump was nearly four feet long and about a foot and a half wide. Each time the flies took their synchronized flight, Noah could see a smooth mottled gray pelt near one end. "I think it's a seal."

As if on cue, the buzzing sound intensified in Noah's head. He covered his ears with his hands as a soft gust of wind grew into a screaming howl, blasting sand in a stinging spray against his face and into his pale blue eyes.

Fighting the urge to turn away, Noah slowly leaned in toward the dark mass, poker held high for protection as he nudged the rotund mound with his foot, hoping the flesh hadn't rotted so much that his foot would sink into it like a hot fork into Jell-O. He silently thanked his mom for nagging him to wear "real shoes" today instead of his usual flip-flops.

As he rocked the body gently with his shoe, the seal lifted its head upward, its bloody mouth agape as it gave out a rattling bark and a gutteral growl that awakened an avalanche of pain inside Noah's skull. The voice bloomed from deep within.

Help us.

Noah jumped back, scrambling crablike away from the creature, nearly knocking Taylor over as he tried to get some distance between himself and the blood-soaked beast.

"Run!" Noah cried. "Get your mom!"

11.

Kate Borcelli leaned in close to examine the torn flesh of the harbor seal, and carefully pushed a gloved finger into one of the long gashes carved into the side of the animal.

The creature took heaving gasps, its nostrils blowing small billows of sand as its eyes scanned the water on the horizon. The seal's breathing became more labored as the marine biologist continued her examination.

"Jeez, what happened to it?" Taylor whispered as she inched closer to the animal, no longer bothered by the putrid smell hovering around it.

"Stay back, Taylor," her mother warned. Her long hair, secured in a ponytail, lashed her face as the wind picked up. Kate's tiny frame teetered precariously next to the creature, her dainty arms extended as she tried to maneuver her metal detector underneath one mottled flipper so she could turn it over for a clearer view of its injuries.

"Is it going to be all right? I mean, can you save it, Mom? It's going to be—"

"Tay—please," her mother snapped. "I'm trying to focus."

Taylor was nonplussed. Noah stood silently watching the two of them volley comments back and forth, his hands shoved deep in his pockets, head down to avoid the blasting sand coming off the dunes. Taylor continued her questions, but now whispering them, thinking that would help.

"What are the gashes? What could cut an animal like that? Will it be all right? How long has it been here? . . ."

Kate quietly ignored her daughter as she continued to prod the animal.

She lightly touched the puss-filled gashes that covered the side of the harbor seal, each soft stroke of her finger punctuated by the animal's heaving sigh, intensifying the sound in Noah's head. He softly swatted at his ears, afraid some of the insects had stowed away in his ear canals and were burrowing toward his brain. He stopped when he saw a kid from school, Kevin Upham, standing next to Taylor. His blue striped board shorts flapped in the wind.

For some reason Kevin had always hated Noah. Noah's mom had tried to get the two of them to play together when they were kindergarteners and Noah had ended up locked in a chest inside a closet while little Kevin laughed about it, holding the key.

The cold air prickled the tiny hairs on Kevin's shirtless chest and he flexed his pectoral muscles in a rhythmic fashion, a goofy grin splitting across his face as he gesticulated at Noah.

Ten other kids from school joined Kevin in a curious semi-circle.

Noah took a step back as the circle tightened, the group pushing him out like they were popping a zit.

Noah stuffed his hands deeper in his sweatshirt pockets, his pale eyes slits of distrust as he watched Jake Stafford approach and gently push aside a group of girls who gathered in a crush around him, like he was some kind of rock star.

Noah almost expected them to ask for his autograph.

Jake moved smoothly, as if he was gliding underwater, graceful but exuding masculinity. Even though he was old enough to be the girls' father, the guy knew he was a chick magnet. Every movement he made seemed to accentuate some muscle group that bulged through his army green shirt and brown cargo pants. He squatted down next to Taylor's mom and the seal, pushing aside a lock of his wavy brown hair. Noah could swear he was trying to flex a bicep as he leaned in to examine the animal.

Using care, he pushed a gloved finger gently into one of the long gashes carved into the large animal's side.

"You found it?" he asked, pointing at Noah, his forearm muscle flexed. The man's green eyes glittered in the morning sun, and Noah could swear he heard one of the girls from his English class sigh behind him. Noah rolled his eyes, exasperated.

"*We* did," Noah said, nodding his head toward Taylor.

"Did you touch anything?"

"No, sir," Noah lied, immediately on the defensive.

"How about you, Taylor?"

Taylor shook her head.

"I think something attacked it," Noah explained, thinking about the words he heard in his head when he found the seal.

"Leave the examination to us, son."

Noah didn't think it was possible to hate the guy more.

Taylor could sense Noah's irritation, and gently nudged him, giving him a warning to keep quiet.

Ignoring her, Noah elbowed his way through the crowd of kids, kneeling next to the seal. "It was attacked."

Stafford glanced up at Noah. "I'm not sure, son."

Noah bristled again at the reference, but pushed on. "I'm not asking you, *sir*. I'm telling you."

"How would *you* know, freak?" Kevin called from behind him.

Turning to face Kevin, Noah's rage bubbled up inside him. "It's true!" he said to Kevin through gritted teeth, walking toward him and jabbing his finger against Kevin's chest, punctuating each of the next three words: "I. Just. Know."

Kevin swatted Noah's hand away. "Get your fish hands off of me," he hissed.

Noah didn't think before he reacted. He shoved Kevin to the ground and vaulted on top of him. The group of onlookers stepped away from the two of them, murmuring a soft chant as they looked on: "Fight, fight, fight, fight . . ."

Before Kevin could fully react, Taylor grabbed Noah by the hood of his sweatshirt, pulling him off. "Stop it, Noah!"

Noah rolled off of Kevin and stood up, dusting the sand off his sweatshirt. Taylor stepped between the two of them. Noah continued glaring at Kevin over her shoulder.

"Come on," Taylor said, pulling Noah away from the crowd. He shrugged Taylor off, hunching his shoulders as they walked down the beach together.

"Your girlfriend can't save you forever!" Kevin screamed weakly from behind them, having lost a bit of his bravado.

Noah desperately wanted to forget the past few days.

"What the heck are you doing?" she whispered to him, doing a quick jog to keep up with his long strides. "I know you're tall, but Kevin is on the football team. He'd pulverize you. Are you crazy?" They could hear Stafford yelling at the kids to get away from the seal, that they needed to go home.

Taylor tentatively touched Noah's arm as she talked, her questions smacking against his skull as she stumbled along next to him. "Come on, just keep walking," Taylor said, steering Noah closer to the bottom of the cliffs that lined the beach.

"Sorry, Tay," Noah mumbled, rubbing his temples to try to push away a newly blossoming pain in his skull. "I just lost it."

"Yeah, no kidding. I've never seen you look so pissed off. My mom and Doc Stafford looked pretty shocked by it all."

"I'm sorry, okay? I just feel like I'm going nuts. I can't get away from the stuff in my head."

"Are you hearing something now?" Taylor asked.

Noah nodded slightly. "It comes and goes. It doesn't make any sense." He ran his hands through his hair, squeezing his temples with his palms, no longer concerned about the extra skin between his fingers. He just wanted the pain to go away. "I swear a voice is saying 'help us,' but I don't know what I'm supposed to do." The pain was evident in his voice. "It's like they're all trying to tell me something—the whales, the fish—but I just don't get what they're saying."

An errant gull cried out, punctuating the loneliness Noah felt as he listened to the waves crash nearby.

"I'm going to go back," Taylor said, nodding toward the group gathered around the seal. "See what's going on. Stay here and cool off." She gently put her hand on his shoulder. "You're going to be okay. We'll figure this out."

"Yeah, I know," he said, although he didn't believe it. As she walked away, it started again. The buzzing began to fill Noah's head. He silently willed it away, prayed for the voices to leave him alone.

From the distance Noah could see the creature taking heaving gasps, its nostrils blowing small billows of sand as its eyes searched the horizon. The inhalations of the seal became more labored, and Noah could tell its lungs were filling up as Taylor's mom and Stafford continued their examination. He knew it didn't look good. And he knew he couldn't do anything about it.

Noah felt defeated. Now Taylor didn't even want to be around him.

He walked closer to the cliffs that towered along the shoreline, hoping for a crevice or cave to hide in, a place to get away from the pain, maybe a place to block what was happening in his head.

As he walked away from the seal, the sound in his head intensified. Nothing was making any sense. Now the sound seemed to come and go even when he was walking away from the seal.

The sound reminded Noah of the leaf blowers the gardeners used in his neighbor's yard. He shook his head violently, trying to clear away the noise. He thought about the seal, about its injuries.

Noah was now more than thirty feet away from the seal, but he still felt connected to it. He was aware of every heaving sigh from the creature. With each sigh, Noah could swear he heard something deep within his head, but he couldn't quite understand it. He concentrated on the tone, the cadence. It was incomprehensible.

Noah somehow knew when the seal breathed its last breath, but the sound in Noah's head didn't stop like it did with the whales. Instead, the sound continued to intensify as he walked toward the cliffs.

His throat felt tight, as if a giant's hand was squeezing it slowly shut, and Noah's head filled with a reverberating hum. He felt nauseous, but like everything he did lately, he pushed the feeling down. There's no way I'm going to toss my cookies out here in front of everyone, he told himself.

He gazed out at the slate gray ocean as the kids from school headed back to their cars. The show was over. The seal was dead. The freak was gone.

Everything was back to normal. Whatever that meant.

A rush of anger resurfaced. Noah tried to push it down, counting slowly to ten as he took long strides away from the dead seal. He could feel the cool sand under his lightweight running shoes and could smell the musty dampness of the limestone cliffs. But as he walked closer to the cliff face, the putrid odor seemed to return.

He wondered if some smells stick in your nostril hair longer—and, if so, why only the really bad ones?

He was about to turn back when he saw it—another large lump closer to the rocks. He silently hoped it was a boulder, but the smell told him differently. As he approached, the familiar acrid aroma stung his nose and brought tears to his eyes.

Then he heard it: the cry of the seal. His brain felt as though it was being cleaved in half and Noah fell to his knees, clutching his head in agony.

In his entire life living in a beach town, he never saw a dead seal, otter or whale. Now it was like they were everywhere. A sense of dread danced up Noah's spine. What the hell was going on?

Heart pounding, teeth clenched, Noah searched the edge of the cliff face, listening for another guttural bark over the shushing sound of the ocean waves. Then the pain was gone. He wondered how many more there were out there. He wondered how many more he would find. How many more times would he be asked for help, but would fall short?

But Noah could tell that the stakes had changed somehow, his drive to figure out how to help ratcheted up a notch.

Unlike the whales or the fish at the pet store, these seals were ripped apart.

12.

Green liquid-filled jars tinkled on the shelves as the lab doors banged open, startling Jake. "Could you be a little more careful with that, Phil?"

The lab tech grunted a reply, pushing the gurney forward, a tarp hanging loosely over one of the seal carcasses. "This thing is heavy as lead. And it stinks."

"Just bring it over to the side of the table next to the other one," Jake barked. "And don't touch it! There have already been too many unprotected hands on these specimens as it is."

"He's being careful," Kate said cautiously from the back of the room, giving Phil a sympathetic smile. "Just put everything in the middle, Phil, near the examination table."

The lab tech pushed the gurney forward, latching it next to a five-foot steel table before exiting the room quickly. "You scare the staff, talking like that," she said to Jake.

"They're all morons," he responded gruffly, obviously in a foul mood. "Once word gets out that the seals washed ashore, your research will stop. You realize that, don't you?"

The phone hanging on the wall began to ring again. It had not stopped ringing since they returned from the beach. Ignoring it, Jake turned his attention to the gurney. "Help me lift this to the table, will you?"

Kate rolled herself over in her chair, taking care to put on fresh latex gloves.

"Not sure what the point is for those," he said, pointing to her gloved hands.

"It's still an investigation, Jake."

"Isn't it obvious to you what did this, Kate?" They shared a silent stare before Jake returned his gaze to one of the seals. "Grab that end and lift on three, okay?"

They hefted the creature onto the table, its cold body making a sickening sound as it came to rest on the cold shiny steel.

"Why are you so sure it was Bessy?" Kate murmured as she began to prod the seal's flesh.

"You should know better than anyone. Don't you still have the scars?"

Kate looked down at her forearm peaking out from underneath her lab coat. Two thin white scars curved in a jagged parallel arc starting from her wrist to the inside of her elbow. "It was an accident. I shouldn't have been so close when feeding her."

"And why did you ever think naming it would be a good idea? I've told you we should never get too close to the subjects when we started this."

"You never said that to me." Kate pushed the sleeve of her coat down, covering the scars. "Besides, she's sweet."

Jake held up one of the flippers on the smaller seal, showing a deep gouge in the mottled flesh. "Does this look sweet to you?"

"Anything could have caused this," Kate said as she examined the pelt more closely, taking measurements between the gashes. "See how the wounds are perfectly symmetrical? The edges clean? It seems more mechanical than organic in nature."

"Kate, you have to stop trying to find excuses for that thing."

"Bessy."

"And stop calling it by a name. It will only make it harder when we have to destroy it."

"We helped bring Bessy into the world," Kate said passionately. "I was connecting with her. I was progressing. You didn't see."

Jake exhaled sharply, tired of the same old argument. "All I saw was a creature that should never have drawn breath." The phone began ringing again, but they both ignored it.

"She understood my commands. And you wanted to euthanize her, all because things didn't go exactly as planned."

Jake looked up at Kate through a curtain of his wavy brown hair. "It was a failure, Kate. *Bessy* was a reject. And you let her go. . . . And now we have to contend with this." He held up the head of a dead seal to punctuate his point.

"It wasn't her," Kate replied in a measured tone, her head held high in defiance. "She would never do something like this. Besides, it's been months. Why now?"

The phone began to ring loudly again. Stafford picked it up, barking into the receiver. He stood with the phone gripped tightly in his hand, the conversation punctuated with an occasional "yeah" and "okay." He hung up the phone and slowly turned to Kate with a look of horror.

"They found something at the beach near Natural Bridges, about a mile from where we found the seals." Jake rubbed his mouth with the back of his hand. "A body . . ."

The color drained from Kate's face. "Another seal?"

Jake took a moment before replying.

"No, Kate. This time it's human."

***

Jake and Kate could see the yellow police tape near the cliff face of the state park flapping a warning to stay clear. The two shared a look of apprehension as they approached the area, walking in unison toward the heavy-set lead detective who lumbered toward them.

"Thanks for coming over so quickly," the detective said amicably. He rubbed the back of his crew cut in an upward fashion. "This is a strange one. Thought you guys could help us out." He pointed to a rocky outcropping. "The body is over there. Found by a local. That's one surfer dude who is going to have nightmares tonight, I'll tell you."

Jake did not want to waste time on chitchat. "What can we do to help?"

"The body has significant wounds. Deep." The detective furrowed his brow as he puzzled through the options of what could have caused it. "At first we thought he was just due to the body pounding against the rocks in the surf, but then we found this inside one of the injuries."

The detective held up a large clear plastic bag in his gloved hand. "This look like anything you've ever seen before?"

Kate gently grabbed the edges of the baggie to get a closer look, turning it slowly as she examined the specimen. The curved claw was approximately six inches long with one serrated edge coming to a sharp point. A small amount of flesh was still attached to one end.

Kate felt a mild sense of revulsion as she envisioned what might have happened to cause this claw to detach. Her voice caught in her throat as she asked, "Where was this found on the body?"

"A gash in the back of the victim's thigh. Why?"

"Just wondering if it might be defensive in nature."

"It seems the wounds wouldn't prove fatal, but the medical examiner will make the final determination. Do you know what this is?" the officer asked, looking more closely at the specimen.

"I . . .uh," Kate stammered.

Jake took a closer look and glanced up at the officer before responding. "We'd have to take it back to the lab for DNA analysis."

"Would you excuse me, please?" Kate asked before slowly stepping away from the two men, arms folded as she looked out at the gentle waves rolling in. She wondered what might have happened out there.

And what would cause it to attack? Would she really do something like that?

Kate thought back to when the pup was born. She was one of their first attempts at a live sea lion birth in captivity. The genetic alterations they had tried to make were supposed to be minor. Increased sonar capability, enhanced brain function, especially in the communication receptors.

She looked over at Jake as he talked to the police officer and remembered how horrified he had been when Bessy was born; how he wanted to destroy it immediately, but she talked him out of it. Again and again. For years she struggled to continue the program; prove that the changes they had made had worked, all the while Jake warned her that they needed to regain control, that their experiment had been a failure and Bessy needed to be neutralized before it was too late.

He only saw the exterior, the deformities. But Kate saw the beauty of their creation—especially when she began to make a connection, began to communicate. She argued with Jake that despite the grotesque features of the creature, the new species would open doors for humanity. Allow a partnership to build between sea creatures and humans. Uncover mysteries of the deep.

She looked across the dunes as the body was carried away in a black bag on a gurney.

Now Jake's worries were being realized.

And it was all her fault.

***

Jake's hands were deep in his pockets, his eyebrows knitted in worry as he shuffled toward Kate, looking more like a kid who had just been scolded than an award-winning geneticist.

"We need to talk," Jake said softly as he guided Kate away from the taped off area. "It needs to stop now."

"What?"

"You know what," Jake replied, a stern look gripping his features. "It's out there. Doing damage," he added, glancing toward the rocky cliffs. "You know how to communicate with it. We can get her back. Contain her."

"I need your word nothing will happen to her."

"Kate, she probably killed that man. Do you realize what that means?" Jake hissed. "She must be destroyed. This all needs to stop. All of it. It was a failure."

"It wasn't. We were—"

"We're going to get out on my boat, you're going to call her, and we're putting an end to this."

"It wasn't her, Jake. I know it wasn't. She wouldn't do that. She must have reacted to something. And she would have never hurt other seals."

Jake looked behind him as the police began winding up the yellow police tape. "Let's talk about this later, back at the lab, away from the police. That's all we need."

"What did you tell them about the claw?"

"I told them the truth," Jake said with a smug grin, his dimples in his cheeks seeming somehow sinister. "I told them I never saw anything like that before in my life."

13.

The wind whistled crazily outside Noah's bedroom window the next morning as he turned the volume up on the small transistor radio. He found it in the pile of earthquake safety supplies in the backyard shed. His mom took his laptop away as punishment for going into the restricted area.

The local weatherman was talking about the storm heading into Santiempo, but he said nothing about the seals they found on the beach the day before.

As Noah spun the dial to find a different station, the voices blended in with the static. He stopped the dial, frozen. The garbled voices mixed with the hissing and popping sounds were almost exactly like the sounds he'd been hearing in his head for the past few days.

Can it be my fillings? He wondered if sound could travel through the metal in your mouth. He slowly ran his tongue over his back molars, fishing for a means of transmission.

Far off voices, muffled and warped, filled his mind. He was almost getting used to these brief interruptions. The sound made him think of the flies—how they moved on the mortally wounded seals.

He remembered watching a documentary about fire ants one time, about how they could connect their bodies together to become a buoyant boat or raft, the bodies working in unison toward a goal of carrying the colony across a body of water.

The flies acted like that yesterday. They had blanketed each seal like a shroud, the black blanket lifting in rippled formation before descending again to feed. What would it feel like to be covered in flies? He shook away the thought.

He tried to focus, but his mind returned to the scene, to the smell and how it had stung his nostrils. The stench had hung with him ever since—even after two showers, three loads of laundry, and a can of air freshener. He pulled at his grey hooded sweatshirt and took a long sniff. The heavy scent of laundry detergent filled his nostrils. No putrid odor of death. That seemed to be coming from somewhere else.

He flipped through the pages of one of his favorite books, *Lessons in Marine Biology*. His mom gave it to him last year when he said he might want to pursue that as a career. She was always doing that; his bookshelves were filled with volumes about the physiology of whales, the migratory habits of sea birds, and anything to do with seals and dolphins—even kelp.

When Noah was ten, he said he liked a play they went to, and she signed him up for a drama class. He said he liked green beans, and she served it for dinner almost every night until he couldn't stand the sight of them anymore. He knew she only did it because she loved him, but deep down he thought it was probably a way to compensate for him not having a dad around.

No father? No problem! Read a book. Eat some beans.

Noah read the caption under a photo of local harbor seals playing in Monterey Bay, explaining how the seals used oxygen underwater:

Pinnipeds have unique blood cells with higher concentrations of hemoglobin (an oxygen bonding protein) and their muscle cells have a higher concentration of myoglobin (another oxygen bonding protein). Their muscles store oxygen when they dive, their heart rate slows, arteries squeeze shut to direct blood flow to the most vital areas, and their pupils expand widely to see better deep under water.

He thought about what life would be like underwater, and wondered if there was a way to up his own myoglobin. Noah jotted down a note on a small yellow rectangle of paper, reminding himself to look into that later. He shoved it into the book as a placeholder.

The book's top edge was lined with similar papers— reminders of other research he planned to do. They made a soft rustling sound as he slid his index finger along their edges, underscoring a feeling of time quickly slipping by.

The wind tossed brittle leaves against the window, startling Noah from his thoughts. The old house creaked in protest. He stood up and took a few steps away from his desk, holding his breath as he listened to the sound as it retreated.

Large oak trees that lined their street danced in the wind, tiny branches scraping the wood siding. Noah returned his gaze to the radio, tuning in a local all-news radio station. The morning newscast was the typical stuff: Santiempo University students returning to class, the city council voting on banning plastic bags, and a few homeless people staging a sit-in near the Boardwalk. Nothing about dead seals. Nothing about beach closures.

In the distance he could see his neighbor, Harold Montgomery, walking his wife's white toy poodle down the block, trying desperately to look macho while the little dog pranced next to him. A large gust sent leaves swirling down the street. Mr. Montgomery grabbed the dog and held it tightly before running, head down, toward his house two doors away.

Noah pushed hard on the wooden window frame to secure it, but he could still hear a small whistle of escaping air. Homes like theirs that were built in the 1920s had all the charm of the time, but lacked insulation and had shifted on their foundations over the years. As he pushed harder to tighten the window in its frame, he saw Taylor jumping up and down on the sidewalk below. His heart leaped a little when he saw her crisscrossing her arms as if directing a jet for landing.

"Come on up!" he mouthed through the window, beckoning her with his arm.

Noah could hear Taylor slam the front door and bound up the stairs. She seemed to do everything in hyper-speed.

The bedroom door flew open, and Taylor stood in the doorway leaning over her knees, panting heavily.

She wore long plaid shorts and a pink sweatshirt with a giant red Elmo on it, a bubble over its head with the words "Elmo loves you!" Silver socks with sparkles rounded out the look with her bright pink running shoes.

"I rode my bike against the wind all the way here," she said, holding up a dainty finger as she worked on catching her breath. Taylor's hair was a spray of tangles. A couple twigs stuck out of the side of her ponytail. "Man, it's crazy out there!"

"Uh . . . you might want to . . . um." Noah touched his head lightly.

Taylor jumped when she saw her refection in the window. She began pulling debris from her hair and dropping it into a nearby wastebasket.

She nodded her head toward the radio with a smile. "Your mom's still got control of the computer, huh? Hear anything?"

"Nothing."

"Why aren't they closing the beaches? It could be a shark out there," Taylor said. "Did you know they just closed the beach at Stinson up past San Francisco? Some Coast Guard guys said they saw a fifteen-footer close to shore."

Sharks were a big concern lately, and it seemed like more attacks were being reported on the California coastline than Noah ever remembered.

"Maybe they're not worried about it."

"Are you kidding me? Those seals were covered in gashes! You'd think they'd at least have a story about it, but I've been watching the news at home, and going online. I heard they found some guy that drowned at Natural Bridges, washed up on shore."

"When did that happen?"

"Last night," Taylor replied as she smoothed her hair down with her palm. "But I haven't heard anything about the seals. It's like it never happened."

"Maybe someone drowning was just more newsworthy. What's your mom say?"

"She's been at the lab ever since yesterday. No word. She even slept there last night," Taylor said as she pulled another twig from a long strand of hair. "My dad was pretty mad. I think they're fighting again."

Part of Noah kind of hoped all of this would go away—the seals, the fish, the whales—and especially the voices in his head.

"You sure there wasn't anything online?" Noah asked.

Taylor plopped herself down on Noah's bed, tightening her running shoes as she talked. "I couldn't see anything except a post from Kevin Upham about how gross it was. He's such a dweeb, by the way. I should have let you kick his ass."

"You said he would have pulverized me," Noah reminded her.

"Well, anyway," Taylor said dismissively with a flick of her wrist. "There's nothing on the Marine Lab website, nothing on the news. Heck, they covered the rats drowning in the estuary—they should be all over this. There's definitely something going on."

Noah thought about everything that had happened over the past few days and thought her comment was one of the bigger understatements she ever made.

From the corner, the radio announcer said, "beachgoers are on alert . . ."

"Quick! Turn it up!" Taylor said, pointing to the radio.

". . . after a homeless man was throwing bottles at tourists near the Santiempo Beach Boardwalk following the annual beach cleanup organized by the city," the announcer continued.

"See what I mean? Nothing about the seals. My mom and Doc Stafford didn't alert the local authorities. Shouldn't they do that? Close the beaches?"

"Maybe not. Maybe it was something natural.

"Or maybe they're just busy with something else . . ."

Taylor looked out the window, watching the trees sway as she processed the information.

"What do you know about the seal we saw at my party; the one in the tank?"

"Why?"

"Just curious," Noah said, not sure about how to bring up the scream he had heard.

Taylor sat on the edge of Noah's bed, smoothing the blue comforter as she mulled through all that had happened. "Can I ask you something? At the beach yesterday, you said to Kevin that you knew the seals were attacked. What did you mean by that?"

"It's just a gut feeling I had. And what I heard in my head." Noah shook his head lightly, trying to remove the memory of the seal staring out to sea. "None of this is making sense," he said softly.

"Well, if you were confused before, you're really not going to like this." She grabbed a folded bunch of papers from her front pocket and handed it over. "It's from my mom's computer, from the other night. I meant to bring it up to you yesterday, but things got crazy."

Another understatement.

Noah saw the words Trident Initiative printed at the top of the first page.

"We have to go back to the lab."

"We can't go back there. We're already in massive trouble."

Taylor held up a small key on her key ring. "I have unlimited access. And my mom's computer is right there in her office."

"Yeah, and so is your mom," Noah pointed out.

"You underestimate me, Noah," Taylor said with a slight grin. "Let's just hope she hasn't changed the locks."

Let's hope she did, Noah thought.

"I think she's working on something more than just communicating with marine mammals, Noah." She shuffled through a few of the pages. "It looks like this Trident project involves messing with DNA. This talks about something called CRISPR technology."

"So?"

"There's a list of names here, Noah." She hesitated before continuing. "Humans, I think."

"Why do you think they're human?"

Taylor pointed to the bottom of the page.

"Because your name's on the list."

14.

Noah was still in shock when they got outside near his garage. Taylor held onto her mountain bike on the leaf-strewn driveway. "Let's swing by Natural Bridges on the way to the lab; scout it out there first."

"Yeah, that's a good idea." Noah pulled his semi-rusted ten-speed mountain bike from a jumble of boxes inside his detached one-car garage. "Less chance of us getting thrown in jail before dinner."

"Don't worry so much, Noah," Taylor said, moving away from her bike and meticulously replacing the fallen boxes in the garage. She flashed a smile his way as she returned to her bike. "You're always such a pessimist."

The garage door hinge protested with a loud shriek as Noah slammed it shut, the warped and splintered wood slab barely locking into place. He engaged a metal bolt on the side of the door and secured it with the sharp click of a heavy padlock. There had been a rash of burglaries in the neighborhood recently, so Noah's mom had enacted new rules about security.

"Where'd you get that key to the lab anyway?" Noah asked. "I thought your mom took that away the other night."

"She did, but I'm not stupid. I always make at least two sets." Taylor jingled a ring filled with keys of all sizes.

"You know you're playing with fire by steeling your mom's keys."

Taylor's smile broadened. "*Found* them, Noah . . . I *found* them, copied them, and returned them. You've got to learn about semantics."

"And you have to learn about plausible deniability and jail terms."

Taylor ignored the sarcasm as they pushed their bikes down the driveway and stopped on the street, waiting for the line of traffic to clear. "Anyway, let's see if there are any signs posted. Maybe someone there will have answers." She playfully jingled the keys a foot away from Noah's face. "You ready to try this?"

He gave a slight nod, but didn't look confident. "You sure this is going to work?" he asked. "How do we get in? What if we get caught?"

"We won't get caught."

"We just *got* caught. Two days ago."

"I'll be more careful this time. I know all the back entrances and I made copies of keys to most of the rooms, too." A wicked smile spread across her face, her eyes crinkled with mischief. "What are they going to do? We'll just get told to leave . . . *again*. I know the drill over there.

It's going to be fine. I'm the grown-up, remember? When have I ever steered you wrong?"

"Aside from when you took me to the Boardwalk after hours and said we could get into the carousel area and ride the horses without permission, and my mom had to pick us up in the security office? Or when you told me one time that if I ate the rind of a pineapple, my face would clear up and I cut the insides of my lip and broke out in a rash? Or when you said that the house on the cliff was haunted, and told me to follow you inside to look at it and we almost got shot by some crazy person who was old as dirt and had a gun that was even older? Or—"

Taylor held up her hand, palm out. "Okay, okay. I get your point."

"But this . . . this just might work," Noah said, shrugging his shoulders with a broad smile. "And it looks like the storm's breaking up, which is a good omen, right?"

He looked for speeding cars, usually filled with sun tan oil-lathered tourists intent on a day at the beach, and not caring who they ran over on the way to get there. On the asphalt, wet leaves flopped in the breeze, reminding Noah of the fish at the aquarium. Soft steam rose from the colorful piles as the rays of sun peeked through the clouds, heating the dampened surface and creating an earthy aroma. He willed the thought of the fish away.

"Let's get this over with," Noah said to Taylor. He pushed off and began pedaling down the bumpy, tree-lined street, weaving his bike tires around the ruts in the road to avoid getting a flat. The center of Noah's street had two metal streetcar rails that had caused a few accidents in the past, so he stayed far to the right.

They shot past old Victorian bungalows with sagging front porches, and others that had been completely refurbished, cornice work redone in bright colors depicting the bygone era.

Noah often thought about what life must have been like in this coastal town back when these homes were built. He always thought it would be cool to drive a horse and buggy. Or just ride on a horse. His mom wasn't a big fan of horseback riding, either. The back of the horse was too high. And there were too many chances the horse would buck you off.

With each intersection, Noah and Taylor could see the bustle of activity just a few blocks to the left on Elm Street, leading down to the main drag of Pacific Avenue. A street fair, its crisp white tents still damp from the recent rain, lined the side streets. They caught a whiff of fried dough and sugar as they sped past.

Noah began to peddle faster, away from his friend.

"Hey, wait up!" Taylor called from behind. Noah was already far ahead and Taylor was becoming just a speck behind him.

He could hear her calling over the wind whistling in his ears. "Come on, Noah! You don't even know how to get in! And I have the keys!"

15.

Jake's tires hit the speed bump hard, rocking the truck as he turned into the parking lot of the Santiempo Marina a few miles south of the marine lab. He glanced at the equipment he and Kate had hurriedly packed in the back of the truck earlier, and hoped he hadn't lost anything. He parked the truck and grabbed two stacked gray plastic containers from the back of the truck and began to walk toward the boat docks.

His Boston Whaler was berthed in the fifth slip at the end, tucked away from the other boats.

"Whachya got there?" The marina owner, Zeke Tisdale, came over and began following Jake as he walked toward his boat. "Loot from a recent burglary?"

Zeke had owned the marina since Jake was a kid, and had caught him breaking into the bait shop when he was twelve, about to steal some fishing poles. Jake's dad was an important man in town, however, so Zeke let it go, but he always made cracks about Jake being a criminal, even after he got his doctorate and started working at the marine lab and winning awards for his research.

Jake picked up his pace, trying to get away from the older man. "Your dog's been barking like crazy," Zeke called after him. "I almost had to go over there to shut him up."

Jake yelled over his shoulder, "Don't go near my boat, Zeke! You know the rules. I have a court order saying you can't come within five hundred feet of my boat."

"I'm just saying you shouldn't leave the dog on the boat by himself." Zeke stopped halfway down the dock, knowing the exact spot where he had to stop. Jake had applied for the restraining order after a recent altercation involving a lot of whiskey going into Zeke and a few threatening words coming out of the marina owner.

"He's fine," Jake yelled over at Zeke as he started to load the tubs onto the deck. Beebo started barking from the cabin of the cruiser, and Jake could see his fireplug of a dog staring out a small window, slobbering on it with each bark. "Beebo, down!"

The dog dropped out of sight, and Jake could hear Beebo's claws clacking on the fiberglass deck, doing a happy dance, so excited to be let out. Zeke was now far away, back at the docks, pumping gas into a waiting boat.

Jake opened the cabin door and Beebo launched at him, stubby tail wagging. Jake pulled the door shut and locked it, watching with a smile as the brown and white English bulldog, all muscle, circled around his legs. "How you doing, boy?" Stafford scratched behind the dog's ears. "You need a little run?"

He hefted the dog over the side onto the dock, and Beebo immediately ran to the first piling he could find and took a whiz on the weathered wooden pole. He began sniffing around as he walked and peed, sniffed, walked and peed some more. Each time the dog's urine stream hit a sunbaked piling, a small curl of steam would rise off the wood.

Zeke was still pumping gas and a rainbow slick rippled on the water. Jake could smell the pungent odor of the fuel as is seeped into the water, and he felt his anger rise. Zeke was always calling himself an environmentalist, talking about the solar power he installed at the marina, or about the cleaner gas he would buy. Then he would let the pumps leak the stuff right into the water. *Nice.*

Hypocrite.   Jake thought the world was filled with them. People who lived so piously, saying they were concerned about the planet, but would run each other over in their SUVs trying to get to a sale on refrigerators at Costco. They won't buy certain types of tuna in a can, but they'll toss their perfectly good appliances or TVs onto the street and buy new ones, instead of fixing what they had, so they can keep up appearances with their neighbors. They go to whale watching tours in their Hummers, driving for miles in a vehicle that gets nine miles per gallon, and heading out on a boat that burns thousands of gallons of fuel a year, so they can snap a selfie of a whale's fluke behind their grinning faces.

Jake glared at the man who he considered another one of the self-deluded tree-huggers. Zeke squinted back at him with a grin.

Zeke was finishing up with the boat when Beebo reached him and started to sniff at the man's leg. "Looks like my dog has taken a fancy to your pants leg, Zeke. I hope you keep an extra pair in your office."

"Call him off, Jake!" Zeke said, pushing the bulldog slightly with his foot. "You shouldn't let your dog roam free like that, and I'm getting complaints about him peeing all over the docks."

Beebo let out a small bark, as if in protest. He returned to sniffing Zeke's tan Dockers and lifting his leg up in little starts, skipping with a tiny limp as he got closer. Stafford laughed. "It's just piss, Zeke. Perfectly natural. A dog has to pee."

"It's not natural for dogs to take a whiz on someone's leg for fun, Jake. And it looks like he's grinning every time he's done it. You teach this thing some manners. Shoo, ya mutt." Zeke pushed the dog away again, and this time Beebo listened. He sat on the dock, looking up at the man as if expecting a treat, his tiny nub of a tail making hollow drumbeats on the dock's wooden planks.

Zeke returned the nozzle and began wiping his hands with a dirty handkerchief.

Jake gave Zeke a tight grin, his green eyes twinkling. "Looks like you're off the hook today."

Zeke looked over at Jake through folds of sun-soaked wrinkles.

"Must be some big thing you're doing going out on the water so much. This must be the fifth time I've seen that type of load in the back." Zeke stared out from under his grimy baseball cap. "Government stuff?"

"Mind your own business, Zeke. You never know. Someday you could end up in one of those tubs on the stern of my boat." Jake gave a knowing wink.

Zeke let out a little bark of a laugh, backing away with his hands up in stick-em-up fashion. "Just saying, is all. Didn't mean nothin' by it." As he shuffled backward heading for the marina office, he called out, "Keep the dog on a leash." Then he slammed the door.

"Moron," Jake said under his breath. He made a mental note to check back with Zeke later.

Beebo was now sniffing at the leg of a tall woman who was obviously uncomfortable with the dog's interest in her faux diamond-studded deck shoes. She held out her jeweled hand, trying to nudge Beebo away with her perfectly manicured fingernails. "Go on, doggie," she mewed. "Go back to your master."

Jake walked over to the woman, but didn't pull Beebo away. He liked to see her squirm. When she saw Jake, her entire demeanor changed. "Is this your dog?" she cooed. "He's cute." Her eyes cut across Jake's broad chest and flicked up to his wavy hair. "What's his name?"

Jake looked at the woman, disgusted by her preening. Even when he scowled, however, women never seemed to notice. They would continue blathering on just to stay close to him. He found it worked to his advantage. And he had fun with it. He found out he could pretty much insult most people right in front of their faces, and if he offered his dazzling white smile and twinkling eyes while doing it, they never caught on. But he wasn't smiling today.

Beebo caught the glare of his master and began to growl softly. The woman waited for Jake to reprimand his dog, but he just stood there. Then he turned and walked back to his boat, leaving her ignored.

Jake smirked as he walked away. He could feel the woman looking at him with a mixture of condescension and loathing, so he turned and stared at her, letting her squirm a bit more before calling out, "Beebo!" nearly scaring the woman off the edge of the dock.

The squat dog barked sharply, adding one last menacingly growl at the woman before racing on his stumpy legs to Jake, who pulled the dog into the boat.

Beebo scratched his paw on the boat's cabin door and Jake unlocked it. He pulled the two tubs into the cabin before slamming the door shut behind him, locking the door from the inside.

As Jake turned the lock, the curtains of the marina office window dropped shut.

16.

Clouds loomed on the horizon, blocking out the sun and turning the water a steely grey as Taylor pulled up next to Noah in the Natural Bridges parking lot. They could see police cars parked closer to the beach entrance. "Must be where they found the body," she said.

Noah could see a darkly streaked curtain of rain falling in the distance. "Storm's coming back. We should go." He honestly didn't want to be anywhere near where a body had washed ashore. It reminded him too much of all the times his mom warned him about water.

They stopped near a tiny trail that meandered along the cliffs through a mobile home park leading to the discovery center and marine lab next door. Five-foot swells smashed into the rocky cliffs below. Blasts of wind kicked up the sea foam, creating a fine mist that sparkled in shafts of sunlight before being carried back out to sea. Taylor tried to gauge how many cars were still in the marine center parking lot. "Doesn't look like a lot of people are over there," she said.

"Off season," mumbled Noah. His thoughts had returned to the gruesome find from yesterday. The memory of the buzzing flies filled his head coupled with the memory of the commanding voice that had boomed inside him.

Help us.

"I don't see signs posted about closing the beaches," Taylor said, squinting down toward the shoreline. "But something's going on."

"We can find out about it later. Come on. Before we get soaked."

Long eucalyptus leaves, the color of weathered wood, kicked up in a crackling wake behind Noah as he sped down the trail. He let his mind wander back to the voices he kept hearing—their deep tonal vibrations, but each unique. The voice he heard at the beach with the seals was more guttural than what he heard with the whales. But the message seemed the same. Why? What did it mean?

His leg muscles burned as he pushed harder, the front wheel slicing into the cool sand on the path. The pounding surf against the cliffs filled him with a sense of urgency; once again, he felt the need for speed. He could hear Taylor calling for him to slow down, but he was entranced, his mind filling with the rhythm of the ocean.

Taylor's voice became a distant whine, like she had been pulled into a long tunnel. Her screams were drowned out by the hum now filling his head. He gripped the handlebars, the skin between his fingers bunching between the digits, making it hard to keep a tight grip as he bumped along the trail. The wind whistled through his hair as he sped up; its roots seemed to almost be pushed upward by the crescendo building inside his skull.

He could smell the coconut oil he used on his hands, mixing with the salty tang in the air. Thanks to a recent growth spurt, he now stood about a foot taller than his classmates. His fingers had grown, too, curving slightly inward at the tips. The webbing between the lower digits was unyielding at times, the fingers encased in the tightly stretched skin, so he had taken to oiling the skin at night like he saw boys do with their baseball gloves to break them in. He now spent hours each night painstakingly rubbing the coconut oil into the skin between his fingers, massaging and flexing, rubbing and clenching until each digit ached.

Whenever his mom came into his room, she would sniff the air and go into a lecture about how tanning oil doesn't protect a person from contracting skin cancer.

"I hope you're using sunscreen, too," she would say as she straightened up the organized clutter around him.

That's the least of my worries, he would think as he stretched his fingers, rubbing the oil in deeper, flexing, retracting.

His bike tires kicked up gravel and more leaves as he turned off of the trail onto Delaware Avenue. He didn't know why he was in such a hurry to get to the marine lab, and his legs burned with the exertion. Shifting gears with the twist of his wrist, he rocketed down the barren street. Empty lots filled with tangles of weeds flanked either side of the pavement.

He hoped he would get to the lab before Taylor. He thought if he was alone, close to the marine life at the lab, maybe he'd finally get some insight into what was going on.

Although he really liked Taylor's enthusiasm, sometimes it was hard to think around her.

She hated silence. And right now, he really needed silence.

No voices in his head.

No intonations.

Nothing.

As he took the turn from Delaware onto Shaffer, he could see the one- and two-story green, weather-beaten wooden buildings of the discovery center. He could hear the waves crashing against the wind-tossed bluffs lining the top of the cliffs just beyond.

Then a blinding scream sliced through Noah's mind, cutting off the sound of anything else.

Noah slammed on his breaks. The bike swerved as the front wheel smacked against a rut in the road. He flew over the handlebars, sailing toward the pitted surface of the asphalt.

Arms outstretched, the flesh shredded from his palms as he landed. The bike slammed on top of him, the front tire slowly spinning. Then he heard it; the voice boomed inside his head.

At first the words didn't make sense; they were a different tone and quality than what he heard at the aquarium, or what had pushed him to the whales.

This time, it seemed foreboding, almost evil.

A warning. *Go back.*

17.

Kate pulled into the marina parking lot and checked her phone to see if she had any messages. Taylor said she was going to hang out with Noah, and she wondered if that was a good idea after finding the seals.

This whole thing had become a nightmare.

Finding the man on the beach and the claw had sent her over the edge, and she wondered how she was going to get out of this.

Taylor would have to take care of herself if there were any problems or her father could always jump in to help, although he had decided to step away from both of them recently, always finding excuses not to come home, or avoiding spending time together, like at Noah's party.

Kate turned off her phone and dropped it into her purse before getting out of her car and walking toward the marina. Jake had wanted to get an early start, but she was hesitant.

What if it wasn't Bessy? Or, worse still, what if it was?

She wondered if she had the guts to find out.

She zipped up her raincoat and increased her speed, her jeans whisking together as her Vans made a hollow thudding sound on the weathered wood.

The Boston Whaler was moored at the end of the dock, rocking softly in the early morning light. Thin wisps of clouds hung in the pale blue sky. She climbed on board and rapped lightly on the cabin door.

"Jake. You in there?"

Beebo let out a sharp bark of excitement and rushed at Kate when Jake opened the door.

"Hey, Beebs," Kate said with a grin, scratching behind the dog's ears. She saw dishes in the tiny sink, the tabletop dropped low, made up as a bed.

She looked up at Jake with a question. "How long have you been living out here?"

"Couple months. Didn't I tell you?" He began to push away bedding, stowing it in the bench seat. "It makes for a good bachelor pad and it's a quick commute to work."

"Yeah. Cozy."

Jake snuck past her and settled into the captain's seat. "You ready for this?"

Kate nodded in resignation, untying the line to the dock.

The boat's engines roared to life and Jake pushed the throttle forward, steering it away from the marina.

"We'll have to do this quickly," he yelled over the engine noise. "The storm seems to be whipping in from the south. We'll only have a small window of time to get her."

Kate's only hope was that once Bessy came to the boat, and they got her back to the lab, she could find a way to save her.

"Do you have the tranquilizer gun?" Kate yelled. "And the harness?"

"Everything's in there," Jake said, pointing with his head toward the main cabin. Beebo jumped onto Jake's lap, paws on the dash in anticipation of the adventure.

"You think it's okay to bring your dog along?" Kate asked.

Jake patted Beebo on the head. "He's our good luck charm. And he can warn us if we get close. Like he used to do at the lab." He scratched the dog behind the ears. "Besides, I don't have anywhere else for him to go."

"Diane wouldn't keep him?"

"We had a bit of a falling out," Jake said as the boat bounced against a large wake. "Beebo will be fine. He can always go in the cabin, if he's trouble."

Kate gave Beebo an assessing look. As much as Jake loved that dog, Kate was never a fan. He used to bring Beebo to the lab, but the dog always seemed threatened by the staff and would sit under Jake's desk and growl and snap at her anytime she walked by, so she had finally asked Jake to leave Beebo home.

The nose of the whaler dropped down as the boat picked up speed. The dog popped his head around the windshield, a giant grin splitting his muzzle as slobber spilled out in a stream behind him.

Gross, Kate thought with disgust.

As if hearing her thoughts, Beebo cocked his head in her direction, ears flattening against his skull as he began to growl.

18.

Noah was surprised to find himself on the ground, blinking up at Taylor who was screaming at him inches away.

"Noah, wake up!"

Her long locks tickled at his face. Noah blinked away the fog in his mind, desperate to remember what happened.

"God, Noah. Are you okay?" Taylor grabbed at the tangled handlebars, pulling the bike away from Noah's crumpled body. She pulled at his shoulders, sitting him up on the road.

"Noah, can you hear me?"

Although he was watching Taylor's mouth move, the ringing in his head continued.

He could feel her hands digging into the flesh of his shoulders, felt his head jostle as she shook him.

"Noah! Snap out of it!"

Go back, the voice croaked once again, now less of a shriek, but still powerful.

Noah winced with its intensity. He looked down at his hands, aware of a growing stinging sensation.

"You're bleeding," Taylor said as she pulled off her zippered sweatshirt, tearing at the fabric and wrapping it around Noah's palms.

"Don't," Noah mumbled, trying to push her busy hands away from his fingers. His pale blue eyes implored her not to touch his fingers and the skin between them. "It's just asphalt burn. It's nothing."

"We have to stop the bleeding," Taylor said as she wrapped one of her sleeves tightly around his left palm, unaware of his confusion.

"I'm okay, Tay."

"No, really. We need to put pressure on the—"

"I said leave it!" Noah screamed, pulling the sweatshirt out of her grasp.

Taylor sat down hard, blinking away the harshness of his outburst. "Just wrap them up yourself then . . . and let's go over to the lab," she said softly. "There's a first aid kit there. Band-Aids."

Noah stared at her, holding the sweatshirt close, hugging it tightly against his chest. He hid his hands in the folds of the soft pink fabric. "I'm sorry, Tay." He wondered if he should tell her why he crashed. If he should tell her about the voice. But it didn't make sense. Go back where? Klamath River? Natural Bridges? Home?

"I think you're in shock," she said. "I read about it. You should cover up." She reached for the sweatshirt, but hesitated, like she was working with a cornered wild animal, unsure if it would strike.

She searched for anything else she could use to wrap around Noah, but there were only empty fields around them. A feeling of isolation loomed heavy.

"Let's get you up," she said, pulling at his arm. "It's just a short walk, Noah. Come on."

As they began to push their bikes toward the weathered green building, Noah's anxiety began to build. This was either a really good idea or an extremely bad one.

He looked behind him at the road leading back home and he wondered if maybe the voice was right.

One thing he knew for sure: He was going to find out how he fit into the Trident Initiative.

***

Noah stood in the parking lot near the discovery center, holding his stinging hands tight against his chest, fighting a wave of fear that coursed through his body. He came to a realization as he stood listening to the crashing waves in the distance. For whatever reason, he was simply different.

The whisperings in his mind were probably going to be part of his life from now on. His hand deformity probably wasn't going to get fixed, and even if he could, the thing about him that made him different was more than his outward appearance. Something was shifting. Changing. And he knew it was out of his control.

The fear morphed to anger, the anger to resolve. Yeah, he was different. But he realized there was a bigger question: What was he going to do about it?

Taylor approached slowly, still a bit apprehensive after Noah screamed at her on the street. She reached out, softly touching his shoulder. "You doing okay?"

He gave her a slight grin, a sense of calm permeating through every cell of his body. "Yeah." He unwound the sweatshirt from his hands and studied his palms. "Looks like the bleeding stopped. Just asphalt burn."

"Well, you should probably put something on it. It'll help take the sting out. The first aid kit is inside, over by my mom's old office."

"By the seal tanks?"

Taylor nodded, looking over at the gate with the warning Authorized Personnel Only.

Noah took a deep breath in preparation, remembering the scream he had heard, the strange creature he saw.

"What's gotten into you?" Taylor asked. "You sure you're okay."

"Listen, Taylor, I don't mean to sound ungrateful, but I'm *not* okay. Based on the last couple of days, I'm either going insane or I'm part of some strange Critter DNA swapping scheme—"

"CRISPR. Not Critter," Taylor corrected. "And it's not DNA swapping. It's a process where you inject a virus into a cell that attacks a specific area of the DNA strand so it elicits—"

"Taylor," Noah interrupted. "It doesn't matter." Noah took a couple seconds, staring at his friend, slowly counting off in his head so he wouldn't completely lose it and start yelling at her. "My point is that I'd really like to get some answers and until I do, I'm going to be a bit nuts. So you need to bear with me and stop asking me if I'm okay."

Taylor twirled her hair, sucking on the tip as she digested what Noah said. "Yeah, I get that."

"Good." Noah let out a cleansing breath. "So let's forget about those bandages and get on with this."

"We should get the bikes out of the way at least," Taylor said. "We might be here a while, and I don't want people to wonder who owns them."

They parked the bikes behind a weathered wooden shed hidden a few feet from the side entrance of the marine lab. The wind began to scream in from the west.

Grains of sand stung Noah's eyes and the now familiar buzz-saw sound returned, pulsing in and out in a slow grinding rhythm. It was happening more frequently now. Taylor seemed oblivious to the noise. Then it cut off.

Noah nodded toward the gate across the parking lot. "C'mon. Let's get this over with."

***

Taylor slowly pushed the gate open, checking the darkened area behind it for any sign of security guards on patrol. With each step, the pea gravel crunching underfoot sounded like shotgun blasts to Noah.

Noah's senses were cranked to their highest level. A trickle of sweat skittered down his neck as they began to lightly run toward the heavy metal entrance door.

The keys loudly jangled in Taylor's hands as she searched for the right one. Noah fought the urge to sprint back to his bike, his eyes large as he continually checked their surroundings.

"Got it!" Taylor whispered excitedly. Noah could tell she wasn't nervous about getting caught. He could tell she was having a blast, while he was stuck pushing down the urge to throw up.

"When we get inside, stay close," she said.

Noah felt as if his skeleton was electrified. Like it wanted to jump out of his skin. The last time they were in this hallway he was overcome by the scream. He anticipated how it would slam into his head as he stepped inside, but when Taylor shut the door Noah didn't hear anything, aside from the slight gurgling of water in the pipes above them. There was no scream of unimaginable horror. Just silence.

"Noah!" Taylor hissed, a few steps away from him. "This way."

Noah had an undeniable sense that something wasn't right.

"Tay—"

The buzzing sound was gone. No screams, no voices. It was as if all the changes that had been happening to Noah over the past couple of days had disappeared. Gone.

The strangest thing about it was that Noah thought it was a bad sign. Isn't that what he had wanted? For this nightmare to end? And now that it seemed like it was over, Noah didn't trust it.

"Something's wrong," he whispered, pulling on Taylor's shirt to get her attention.

They were stopped in front of the door to the restricted area—the area with the tanks and the seal. "We have to check in there."

"Are you hearing the voices again?"

"That's what's weird. I'm not hearing anything at all."

Taylor could tell Noah wasn't in the mood to argue, so she pulled out the keys and began searching for the right one. The lock clicked open, the sound echoing off the dark gray walls. Noah quickly stepped inside, rushing over to the tank, no longer fearful of the creature he saw the other night.

Concern washed over him as he looked over the tank's edge.

It was empty.

19.

Beebo sat perched on the white leather bench seat lining the Boston Whaler's bow, his small ears flapping joyously as the wind blasted the dog's short brown fur. Jake sat in one of the two swivel captain's chairs next to the cabin door in the middle flagship area.

Jake had always liked boats. During graduate school he lived on the boat with his first dog, Perro, in the small cabin under the wheelhouse. It was close quarters, but with a small bathroom and galley with refrigerator and microwave, the Boston Whaler fit their needs at the time. It was coming in handy now, too, and was serving a larger purpose.

Kate exited the cabin and sat on the chair next to him. A strong breeze carried strings of drool from Beebo's mouth out to sea, his jowls making a soft slapping sound as the loose flesh lightly pounded the dog's skull. The wind made it tricky to maneuver the boat as Jake steered it between the sailboats and cruisers docked at the harbor.

Jake remembered when a small tsunami hit the Santiempo Harbor and a lot of the same boats he was passing were tossed onto the docks like bath toys. He had lucked out; the tsunami hit right after Jake had pulled his boat from the water for servicing.

As they left the five-mile marker just outside the boat slips, Jake yelled for Kate to hold on. Beebo ran to his master and plopped himself between Jake's legs.

The twin engines roared as the boat rocked, taking each jolting wave as they headed out past the five-mile-per-hour marker. Beebos's stubby legs dug into the white leather cushions, seeking balance with each bounce the hull made against the wakes.

Kate grabbed a hat from under a glove compartment and stuffed her long hair into it, pulling down the brim to shield her eyes from the wind.

"Where are we heading?" Jake yelled.

"Out past Seal Rock," Kate screamed over the roar of the engines. "Between there and Natural Bridges."

"Won't that be a bit too close to shore?"

"It's got to be fairly close or the man they found would have been pulled out to sea."

Kate held the hat on the top of her head with one hand, and held on with the other as the cruiser bounced through the rough waves. "I still don't believe she attacked him; it's not like—"

"We just need to find it; check if it has a missing claw," Jake screamed, pushing harder on the throttle. He reveled in the speed, the hunt. "Once we stop, you can start to call it."

Kate nodded slightly, setting her jaw as she thought about the next steps, wondering if it may be too late. If Bessy had become assimilated to the open ocean, would she recognize the call out here? Kate had been able to communicate with her at the lab using an oar banging against the tank wall. She wondered if banging on the side of the boat would transmit the sound adequately.

Part of her hoped it wouldn't.

Kate looked off at the vast expanse of the ocean with trepidation. Pewter clouds hung heavy; a fine curtain of rain fell in the distance. They wouldn't have much time before the storm hit.

A salty mist sprayed into the air each time the bow of the boat smashed against a wake. As they headed out past Seal Rock, Jake slowed the boat down to look for the ten-mile marker.

Beebo growled and began to bark.

Maybe Jake was right to bring that dumb dog after all, Kate mused. Beebo jumped off the bench seat, his curved nails slipping on the slick fiberglass surface before Jake grabbed the dog as he skidded past. Jake propped him in his lap, but the dog continued to bark and growl, looking out at the choppy water.

She's close.

Kate slowly began to tap the side of the hull with the wooden oar, then sliding it along the fiberglass bow. Tap, tap tap . . . slide. Tap, tap tap … slide.

Come.

20.

"Where did it go?" Noah asked. "This is the right tank, isn't it?"

"There's nothing in there?" Taylor joined him on the stepladder to see inside the tank. She looked around the room, as if she would find the seal playing some sinister game of hide-and-seek, undetected under a desk or behind a cabinet.

"That explains why I wasn't hearing anything," Noah mumbled lightly to himself.

"What were you hearing before?"

"It was a scream." He suddenly made a connection; the scream he heard on the way to the lab, before he crashed his bike was similar. He wondered why he hadn't realized that before. Then he remembered what the voice told him after he heard the scream: *Go back*. Maybe it wasn't a warning to go home; maybe it was a warning to come here. To help.

"Earth to Noah." Taylor put her hand on Noah's shoulder, concern spreading over her face. "What's going on? You look like you're ten miles away."

The silence in his head now seemed deafening. "We have to find out what your mom was working on in here. There's something I have to do."

"What?"

"I have no idea." Noah looked into the empty tank, hoping to will a message from the ceiling lights reflecting off the water. "Which way to your mom's office?"

Taylor stepped off the ladder, motioning Noah to follow. She quietly opened the large metal door and peered outside.

"All clear," she said softly. "Follow me."

***

Jake wandered to the boat's stern and felt under a tarp near the long bench seat. The tarp hid a large harpoon gun ending in a two-foot-long spear. He opened the top of one of the containers and a whiff of rotted fish hit him full-force. "God, this is disgusting," he said as he gulped sea air into his lungs. The mounds of smelly flesh had begun to cook in their putrid juices.

Kate held the bottom of her jacket against her nose and mouth as she looked at the seal's remains. A seagull cried out in the distance followed by several others. Soon the air above his boat was filled with the white and grey birds hovering above the boat's smelly hull.

"What are you going to do with that?" Kate asked.

"*We* are going to dump it, Kate." He pointed to the two other tubs secured next to it. "And those, too."

"I never agreed to dumping anything in the ocean."

Jake stood up straight, pulling out his harpoon gun. He glared at her, holding the weapon at a menacing angle. "Things have changed a bit since we first started this, Kate. Your controlled experiment? It's out of control. Once you let that thing loose, and it started killing people, all bets were off."

"You were going to kill her."

"She was a freak of nature, Kate. Your creation, I admit, but still a freak." Jake pulled the lip of the plastic container closer to the boat's edge and took out a large metal gardening trowel from below a seat, then started putting on heavy-duty plastic gloves. "I'll start shoveling. You call her."

"I won't do it."

Jake leaned in so close to Kate, she could smell the peppermint gum he was chewing. "Listen," he said. "You put me in a tight spot. We need to do damage control and you're going to help by calling that thing to us, so we can take care of it. We're getting rid of everything. It's over. I know it comes to you when you tap the paddle, so start tapping."

"I won't—"

"You will," he snarled, grabbing her arm tightly, "because if you don't, there is going to be trouble. More trouble than you could have imagined when you set out to save the planet."

Kate saw her backpack leaning against one of the bench seats. If she could only get to it, reach the pocket on the right side, she could get her cell phone, call for help. She dove for it, screaming, "I'd rather go to jail."

Jake was quick to respond, grabbing her by the back of her shirt as she fought for a grasp of the large padded strap. "You don't get to decide anymore, Kate. It's too late for that. We're way too far down the rabbit hole now. So if you're not with us—" Jake shoved her toward the cabin. "You're against—"

Kate swung the backpack hard. She used the pack for dives, and knew the contents were heavy, but she hoped they were heavy enough to do some damage. She swung it at Jake's head, but it whistled in the wind above him as he ducked away. The pack was too heavy, the momentum too strong; it flew over the side of the boat, pulling Kate in with it, smacking her head sharply on the metal boat cleat before she went over the side.

There was no cry for help, no thrashing in a desperate attempt to stay afloat.

She simply silently sank below the surface. Gone.

Jake screamed for Kate, searching the water for any sign of her. Nothing. He looked around to see if there were any other boats around. He was alone. A swarm of seagulls hovered overhead, screaming in protest, and Beebo barked at them enthusiastically.

"Shut up, Beebo!" Jake screamed. He needed silence but those damn birds wouldn't shut up. Jake's head felt like it was going to explode. He needed to think.

He looked at the empty life preserver sitting languidly in a half inch of water on the boat's deck and considered his options. The gulls continued their cries, but Beebo watched his master with curiosity, silent. Finally, Jake returned to the tub and continued to dig out its contents with quick thrusts that penetrated the soft mound, scooping out large handful-sized portions before plopping them gently over the side where his colleague had been just seconds before.

The water turned murky with blood. Jake wondered how soon before the sharks arrived.

Beebo looked on with dull interest, the smell keeping him back. The wind picked up and forced the noxious odor into Jake's nostrils, but he pushed on. Time was no longer his friend. He needed to get back to the lab and clock in. He needed a plan.

He looked off toward the homes dotting the cliffs along the shoreline, sunlight winking against large plate glass windows that faced the ocean. The beauty of the coastline used to take his breath away—make him happy to be alive. Now he felt nothing. All he saw was a crush of people on the beaches, the lines of cars honking along the coastal roads, their exhaust clogging the air.

They're like locusts, he thought.

He tossed another chunk into the water and checked the fish finding monitor once again. Shafts of bright sunlight pierced the storm clouds in the distance; Jake squinted to look for any sign of life on the sun-speckled ocean. Nothing.

About fifty yards away, a V-shaped wedge of brown pelicans flew low near the water, their dark forms reflected along its surface as they searched the depths for prey. Sea gulls continued to cry from above, hovering at various heights as if suspended on strings, surveying the boat for any potential food source.

He turned away as he poured the remaining contents of the container overboard, the smell still overpowering. The seagulls hovered closer, their screams accelerating as they jockeyed for pieces of flesh floating on the surface.

"You should all be exterminated like the vermin you are," Jake mumbled as he finished cleaning out the empty containers, pouring sea water into them with a large measuring cup, swishing the sludge around and dumping it over the side.

He packed his harpoon gun into the case and set to work securing the containers for the trip home.

As he knelt down to grab the rope that had become tangled under seats, he saw a pelican dip down low about twenty feet away to investigate a shadow hovering just inches below the water's surface.

Then, as if being turned off by a light switch, the pelican was gone.

The fish finder alarm began to sound. Beebo rumbled a low growl.

It was close.

Jake pulled out the harpoon gun and looked through the viewfinder, searching the water surface for his target. Then, just as quickly as it had started, the alarm stopped.

The creature was gone.

21.

Taylor pulled Noah back into a darkened hallway near an exit sign and peaked around a corner.

"Looks like the coast is clear. Come on."

"You sure this is okay?"

"Don't worry so much, Noah. I do this all the time," she whispered as she used one of the keys to unlock the door and slipped her thin frame through a small opening. "Make sure to duck around the first corner quick so the cameras don't capture your image."

"*This* is what I'm talking about—" he started to say, but Taylor was already through the passage. Noah took a deep breath and pushed through the opening, quickly dropping to his knees.

"Shut the door behind you," Taylor whispered, "but make sure you don't slam it. The specimen jars in people's offices rattle when you do," she added, pointing to a couple closed office doors on the right side of the hallway.

Noah shut the door quietly, and inched over to her. "This doesn't seem like a good idea. Isn't there a simpler way to get over there?"

"Just keep cool and we'll be fine."

Noah let go of a big puff of air, not realizing he had been holding his breath.

"Come on," Taylor whispered, moving farther down the hall. "My mom's office is just down there."

***

The two of them ducked inside the office and Taylor quietly shut the door, making sure the latch was secure. She did it so slowly that Noah thought it would swing back open on its own. "You sure it's locked?"

"Yeah, they can't get in."

"Security cameras?" Noah asked, looking in the corners of the office.

"Skeleton crew until 5 p.m., and they're lazy," Taylor said as she slowly opened and shut drawers on the desk along the far wall. "One time I was in here until almost ten o'clock, and they never came by to check. They just walk the halls and I've even seen some of them hiding headphones while they listen to Giants games."

"What about your mom and Dr. Stafford?"

"Their cars weren't in the parking lot. We should be safe for a while."

Noah didn't like the sound of that. How long is "a while"?

Taylor moved to the other side of the office, wheeling her chair slowly across the floor to a bank of file cabinets.

"We didn't open these file drawers when we searched before because Doc Stafford didn't have my mom's keys, so let's start there."

"What are we looking for?"

"Exactly what we want: answers." Taylor slowly began to open the top drawer of the metal filing cabinet next to the silver lab table, flipping through manila folders, searching for something that might stand out.

Noah sat at the computer and typed in the password they used earlier. The Trident Initiative data popped onto the screen. He scrolled down, speed-reading the text as he did, trying to make sense of the information.

"Print the last page," Taylor whispered. "We need to get out of here."

The printer whined loudly as it began to warm up. Noah willed it to be quiet, staring out the door's window with mounting apprehension as Taylor quietly grabbed each page and began scanning the information.

Noah's heartbeat was now a battle thrum, his neck pulsing with the rapid rhythm. A shadow crossed his line of vision at the end of the hallway.

"Crap! Someone's coming!"

"Turn off the light! Under here, quick!" Taylor waved for Noah to join her under the metal table.

They could hear footsteps approach and stop outside of the door.

"The printer!" Noah hissed.

"Shhh," Taylor said, her finger up to her lips. They both looked at the printer, its green light flashing, telling the user that more pages were being queued.

"It's going to go again," Noah said softly, his heart slamming inside his chest. He could hear the blood rushing in and out of his carotid artery. A thin line of sweat formed on his lip as he stared at the printer, hoping it would malfunction.

"I think . . ."

"Quiet," Taylor whispered. "Listen. Footsteps." They saw a shadow pass across the small window in the doorway, and heard the footfalls of large shoes echoing off the concrete floor, retreating.

Noah looked at Taylor, and leaned against the back wall, trying to use the cement bricks to cool his body. "We have to get out of here."

"Yeah, let's go." Taylor inched out from under the table, holding the printed sheets tightly in one hand. "We have enough here to keep us busy."

The printer hummed to life. Taylor grabbed the cord and yanked, cutting the machine mid-print. "Grab that paper," she said to Noah. "Come on." She closed out the computer, returned the files, and motioned for Noah to follow her.

The wind whipped through the nearly empty parking lot, scattering leaves and gravel as Taylor and Noah hunkered behind the wooden fence that hid their bikes. The uncertain weather had driven off the tourists, for the most part, so they were less worried about being discovered. They could hear the crashing waves in the distance, and an occasional seal barking from one of the tanks nearby.

Now sheltered from the wind, Noah could smell a hint of apple from Taylor's shampoo.

"Have I ever told you about my mom's work?" Taylor asked. "I mean her real work? What she was really passionate about?"

"I knew she worked on environmental issues, and the effects of water pollution on marine mammals. Why?"

"My mom was getting pretty intense about sea level rise and climate change. She even wanted us to sell our house because she was convinced it would be under water in about six years. Said we should move to higher ground. She wanted to stop ocean dumping and thought corporations, landfills and pollutants were contaminating the food web. She started speaking at conventions, contacting Congress, and coordinating protests at land fills. Did you ever go to any of those?"

Noah shook his head. "Uh-uh."

"She was convinced they were polluting our oceans and groundwater."

"So? She's not the only one who thinks that."

"Yeah, but I bet she was one of a few people out there who thought she could do something about it."

Taylor started flipping through the printed pages in her hand.

"There's something weird about this stuff," she said. "This information seems to focus more on the levels of contaminants and not on what they're finding in seals. See?"

Taylor pointed to a graph that seemed to chart increasing levels of DDT applied over time.

"How could she track levels of a chemical over time?" Noah asked. "I thought they were just taking samples from local marine life, checking for anything in the water that might be hurting the animals." Noah pointed to the bottom of the page. "This actually charts specific units."

Taylor scooted closer, the smell of her apple shampoo nearly overpowering Noah as he read on. "They'd have to be adding the stuff themselves to know that. Poisoning them on purpose."

Taylor looked at Noah, her eyes glistening. "Why would they do that to the seals?"

"You'd have to ask your mom."

Taylor flipped the pages to one with several photographs of a seal; at least Noah thought it was a seal. It reminded him of the one he saw in the restricted area. The flesh was a mottled green that looked like some kind of slime kids could buy in a toy store. The eyes of the animals were bulging, the irises red, the size of silver dollars. And the jutting jaws were like nothing he'd seen on a marine mammal, outside of a horror film: jagged, and tangled, each tooth looked about six-inches long.

"You think the chemicals could cause this?" Noah asked. "You think she really did this on purpose?"

"I don't know," Taylor said with a wistful expression.

She pulled out her cell phone and flipped to a couple pictures from the beach the day before. "These are the seals we found. Look at the gashes. You think one of these deformed seals could do that?"

"I guess so. But why would they kill their own species?"

"I don't know. Maybe the chemicals cause more than just a deformity. Maybe it makes them a little crazy."

"But why would your mom release something like that into the wild?" Noah thought about the scream that had filled his mind and about the warning he had heard on the way to the lab. He lightly touched the asphalt burn on his palms.

Taylor continued to stare at her phone. "Did I ever tell you what she was hoping to discover?"

"Not really."

"She was researching the effects of methylmercury and organochlorines on sea life," said Taylor.

"Organo—?"

"DDT is an example of an organochlorine."

"I'm not even going to ask how you know that," Noah said.

"My mom forced me to do my own research on the subject. Said it would be good for me," Taylor explained. "Others included polychlorinated biphenyls – PCBs – and dioxins. The electrical industry used PCBs as insulators, at least until people realized how toxic it was and what an environmental threat they posed. That was back in the mid-1970s."

"The dark ages," Noah chimed in.

"Yeah, right. Dioxins are the most potent chemical carcinogens known. They get into the environment when companies do stuff like bleach paper white."

"So what does that have to do with the seals?"

"When organochlorines enter and go higher in the food web, they have a tendency to reach progressively higher concentrations, something she said is called biomagnification," Taylor softly explained. "Maybe these seals were a new species—a mutation caused by the chemicals being dumped in the ocean."

"But I thought you said that one seal was born here."

There was a long silence before Taylor continued. "One time I told my mom she should try to get legislation passed, but she just kind of laughed at that. She would have never laughed about something like that before. She was always writing letters to Congress about environmental issues. And she used to take me to the lab all the time, but for the past year she just kind of stopped. A couple months ago I snuck over here anyway. Tried to see what she was doing.

"I knew the saltwater tanks were open to the air and I could see them from the viewing deck, but when I got there everyone was scrambling around, like it was some kind of disaster drill or something, and one of the tanks was covered with a black tarp. After that, they changed the locks and they added keypads with passwords on some of the doors. I tried to ask my mom about it, but she totally shut me down.

"She started spending days and nights at the lab," Taylor said quietly as she fumbled with the stack of printed pages. A tear tracked down her cheek and Noah fought the urge to wipe it away. "If I called her to talk, she was always too busy. She even slept at the lab sometimes and she would go on long research expeditions with her team. A few months ago she started going out for nights at a time on dives that she could never tell me anything about. I just thought she was leaving my dad, like they were going to get a divorce or something.

"That's when I started recording her phone conversations." She pulled out the small digital recorder from the front pocket of her backpack. "Remember this?"

"That's what you were going to use the other night. At the tank."

Taylor gave a half grin. "I was pretty much hiding everywhere back then, recording everything, but once they found out what I was doing, my mom and dad started talking in code, and they'd check the desks and closets before talking about anything important." She shoved the recorder back in the zippered pocket. "I know I did it to myself, but I still felt shut out. A fishing tour boat found one of the deformed seals a few miles outside of Natural Bridges a couple of weeks later. It was this one," Taylor said, pointing to one of the photos in the stack. "The one with the misshapen flippers that had to push its lumpy body toward the surface for air. That's the one you saw the other night in the tank.

"But I just knew about two seals at the lab," Taylor said. "This Trident Initiative seems to imply there were a bunch more."

"You think they were born here, with deformities? Forced mutations?"

"That's what it looks like." Taylor and Noah shared a moment of clarity and dread.

Then Noah pointed at his chest.

"And I'm one of them."

22.

Jake pulled into the marine lab parking lot and shut off the engine. He looked at himself in the mirror and smoothed his hair, combing the thick waves with his fingers.

Stay calm, he told himself.

It had been a couple of hours since he ate the bowl of oatmeal for breakfast and his stomach grumbled in protest. He thought through what had happened on the boat and what he was going to say when people started asking questions. They always asked questions. Jake looked for answers in his reflection, took a deep breath and opened the door of the truck.

Fortunately the lot was nearly empty. It was his favorite time at the lab; when he had the place to himself: no tourists asking dumb questions about the lifecycle of a sperm whale or how starfish eat.

Jake stacked the three plastic containers, now filled with water samples in jars that tinkled together as he walked. He noticed two bikes tucked behind the dumpster and made a mental note to check on that when he left.

Jake's footfalls echoed off the stark cement walls as he made his way to Kate's office—or now it was his office, wasn't it? He was already getting used to the idea that Kate was gone and he would be the one in charge. A smile spread across his face, dimples sinking deep as he unlocked the door, flipped on the lights, and went inside. He thought about Phil, the lab tech, and how freaked out he was going to be when he heard that Jake was now in charge.

The swivel chair squeaked in protest as he sat down and wheeled himself closer to the specimens located on metal shelves along one wall.

The smell of antiseptic was heavy in the air. Sterile. Every surface scrubbed and shiny, waiting for the next piece of flesh to be eviscerated, studied. This is how it will be from now on. Perfection.

A photo of Kate, Taylor and Nick Borcelli sat in a metal frame, Kate's accusatory eyes smiling at him. He flipped the frame face down and rubbed his neck, trying to push away a knot in the muscle and a blooming headache.

He pushed away from the lab table, and took a deep breath, stretching his arms high above his head and cracking his knuckles. He was tired of inhaling the fumes of death and decay. He looked forward to getting home, relaxing, cracking a beer and watching some baseball. Forget about the day. Forget about Kate. A story began to bloom in his mind. He picked up the phone and dialed the security desk.

They answered on the first ring. "Can I help you, Dr. Stafford?"

"I was just wondering if you had seen Dr. Borcelli recently. We had an appointment at Natural Bridges earlier and were supposed to meet here afterward, but she isn't here."

"No sir, we haven't seen her on site, but we'll let you know when she arrives."

"Thank you," he said and hung up the phone. He checked his watch, noting it was nearly one o'clock. A gust of wind kicked up, peppering the side of the building with pea gravel.

He took a pair of tweezers and dropped a tiny piece of flesh onto a glass microscope slide and slowly spun the small dial on the side of the microscope to sharpen the focus. He pulled out a notepad from his backpack and jotted a few things down before leaning back and rubbing his eyes, trying to clear the memory of Kate sinking into the water.

What was he going to do? People had seen her get on his boat at the marina. Jake grabbed a specimen jar for closer inspection. Think, Jake, think.

He wiggled it and watched the contents float in the liquid.

He reached over to turn on an overhead light and noticed the printer cord unplugged on the floor.

Jake returned the specimen to the jar, and lifted the receiver to his face, cradling it between his cheek and shoulder as he leaned under the desk to plug in the printer. The security officer picked up on the third ring, just as the printer sprang to life.

"Hey, Frank. It's Doctor Stafford again." Jake watched as the printer spit out the final page of the Trident Initiative. "Can you check the tape and tell me if anyone was in the office while I was out?"

"It might take a while," the security officer said.

Jake crumpled the piece of paper that the printer had spit out. He thought of the bikes parked near the dumpster, and immediately realized who had been there.

23.

Noah knew they were busted by the way the gate slammed shut, the approaching footsteps quick, heavy, and determined. "Check the tanks," one security guard told the other. "Check everywhere."

Taylor grabbed the pages and stuffed them in her backpack. "Out that way," she said, motioning her head toward a side door across the parking lot as she shrugged the backpack onto one shoulder.

They ran low to the ground and entered a dark hallway. Taylor shut the side door quietly behind her, motioning for Noah to follow. They wound around the corridor, glued to the walls as they inched along, breathing through their open mouths to avoid even the slight nostril hiss. Taylor pointed toward a darkened exit on the far side of the building. "This way," she whispered. They quickly ran across the gravel road to the back entrance of the Discovery Center.

"Over here," Taylor said, pulling Noah's jacket into a darkened area near the back door and pulling out her large key ring.

"Hurry up, Tay. I think I see someone coming." The early afternoon sunlight cast shadows around every corner. Noah felt his insides churn. He willed himself to breathe slowly as he watched Taylor search. His heart hammered in his throat, making him feel lightheaded.

Try to focus. Stay cool.

Taylor held up a ring of keys, the jingling sounding more like a burglar alarm to Noah than the tinkling of bells.

"This one!" she said, holding up a dark blue key. "I color coded them for easier reference."

Noah wheeled his hand in a hurry-up motion. "You're going to make an excellent crook, Taylor. Now get moving." He could swear he heard voices on the other side of the wall. "You sure this place is closed? You hear that?"

Taylor put the key in the lock and turned it slowly. "It's Sunday. There should only the cleaning crew and a couple of security guards wandering around. Come on."

***

He was doing it again. Noah stopped clenching his hands long enough to wipe his sweaty palms on his pants. Taylor tapped him on the shoulder, whispering, "Earth to Noah . . ."

"Just listening to the ocean and trying to figure out a plan," Noah replied. The air had an acrid taste to it, salty with a hint of something else. Can you taste fear?

Taylor crawled to the opening between the fence and the dumpster, checking to be sure they hadn't been noticed.

Noah scooted in next to her. "Can you get us into the dolphin tanks?"

"Sure. I know a back way in. Oh, and I have an idea. She rummaged through her backpack, pulled out a plastic baggie with a few Cheez-It crumbs in the bottom, dumped them onto the ground and dropped in the digital recorder, securing the top with her ponytail holder and shaking it upside down to make sure it was secure. Then she pulled out some duct tape and wound it tightly around the opening.

Nick looked on in wonder. "What else do you have in that backpack?"

"You'd be amazed." She shook the baggie in front of Noah playfully. "Water proof," she added with a wink. "Wouldn't it be cool if we can catch them talking? You know, like the ghost hunters catch ghosts talking with these things. Maybe they speak on a different frequency than we do. You know . . . like you said. Radio waves. I have a software program at home that can—"

"You're not going to stick that in the water with the dolphins, are you?" Noah's harsh whisper reverberated off the walls. "What if there's a leak? It could short out and hurt them."

"Relax. There's hardly enough charge in this to electrocute them or anything. I've tried it before in the bathtub, but you have to use these heavy-duty freezer bags. This duct tape is amazing stuff. I was trying to see if I could record my voice under water one time, and it came out okay. I made a few adjustments to the volume controls, but it's really cool once you download it. It sounds kind of—"

"Let's talk about it later," Noah whispered, not even wanting to ask why she'd want to record herself singing underwater in the first place, let alone discussing how dangerous that was. He hated to admit it, but he was starting to think like his mother. "We have to go before we get caught out here, okay?"

Taylor stuffed the recorder into her pants pocket and gave Noah the thumbs up sign. Then without any hesitation, she started out. As he followed her, Noah wondered what he was really getting them into.

"Come on," Taylor whispered behind her, motioning with her head as she slowly crept across the parking lot, the sunlight glinting off of the small pieces of gravel, reminding Noah of the fish scales reflecting the overhead lights as they flopped around dying on the floor after jumping from their tanks.

"Come on, hurry up," she whispered, motioning to Noah with one hand.

Noah's skin prickled in the cool afternoon air. The sky was filling with ominous dark gray clouds, the sun sliding behind them and lighting up their edges in a brilliant white. Seagulls screeched in the distance, and Noah's internal alarm bells started to ring loudly. He had ignored his misgivings about doing this type of thing before, and it had landed him in his room for a week.

Was this really a good idea?

Noah hated getting into trouble, and this whole thing reeked of trouble—the stink to high heaven kind of trouble that would cost him big, if his mom ever found out.

Noah had always felt an incredible sense of responsibility to not draw attention to himself and to make things easy for his mom. He guessed it was because he never wanted people to feel sorry for him. He remembered one time he got caught taking a piece of candy from a grocery store without paying for it, and his mom had marched him back into the store, and made him apologize to the manager.

The manager thought he was being incredibly nice, saying he appreciated the apology, and no harm done. All

Noah saw was the man continually looking down at Noah's hands as he talked, then looking at his mom in what Noah determined to be a mix of pity and disgust.

For Noah, staying out of trouble gave him a bit of invisibility.

Unfortunately, Taylor's approach to life was exactly the opposite, and in the past he didn't have the guts to tell Taylor no, since she basically was his only friend—and, he admitted to himself, getting into trouble with Taylor was usually a lot of fun.

But this time was different.

This time he knew it was the right thing to do.

Taylor motioned to Noah again, whispering, "Over there." She pointed to a door left slightly ajar near barrels stacked next to the garbage bins. "My mom locked herself out one time, and had to go all the way around to the front with fish guts covering her apron, so she always kept this gate unlocked," Taylor whispered softly. "Looks like they were just here. The door's not even closed all the way. It's our lucky day."

Noah groaned inwardly. "Don't jinx us," he said.

He'd lost count of how many times Taylor had said it was their lucky day and how many times it was followed by a one-hour lecture from his mom about responsibility.

The gated fence housed several buildings as well as a giant water tank that pumped salt water from the ocean into the dolphin and seal enclosures located outside the research buildings.

"Hurry up," she whispered, motioning him closer with quick strokes of her hand. "They lock it after the last tour."

Noah blew out a large gush of air and headed her way, walking deftly on the gravel to soften the sound of his flip-flops snapping loudly against his heals.

"Once we're in there, and they lock it, how do we get out?" Noah whispered sharply. But he was talking to empty air; his friend was already inside, the gate swinging slowly shut behind her. He grabbed at it quickly before it could bang against the frame and alert someone, then he quietly eased the gate shut behind him as he entered the yard.

As they walked, they stayed close to the building, trying to step as lightly as possible and not disturb the gravel on the ground. Each step sounded like gunshots to Noah, as his feet nestled into the tiny chunks of rock. Noah felt like his head was being filled with helium, the pressure inside building.

The buzzing returned as they rounded the corner. It was the first time he felt comforted by the sound. He had started to fear that he wouldn't hear the buzzing again, that the voices would go away and he would never find out the answers.

Then it all came back.

His left ear was the worst, as if hundreds of bees were smashed into the hollows of his ear canal. He could tell that Taylor was saying something, but the din made her voice seem to sputter in and out.

Nothing made sense.

"I—then you—when they're—until it's time," he heard her say.

"What?" he whispered loudly, digging the knuckle of his left hand into his ear.

Taylor's finger shot up to her lips, as she mouthed her response. "Shhh . . . Be quiet." She pointed at a ramp leading up on the right. Then he heard it: the muffled conversation of two adults. The buzzing made it difficult to know who it was, and if it was safe.

Leaning in close to Noah's ear, Taylor whispered, "I'll check to see if the coast is clear."

Before he could object, she was gone.

He felt completely exposed as he pushed himself into the side of the building, trying to become part of the damp wood siding. He knew they were close to the tanks because he could hear the chatter of the dolphins.

Come on, Taylor . . . where are you?

Fear gripped him; it felt like his feet were encased in cement. His intuition told him to keep moving. He knew security guards were close by, but he felt disoriented with the churning sound in his head.

Still hugging the wall, Noah inched closer to where he could hear the squeaks and whistles of two dolphins. He spotted Taylor hunched down next to the tank, beckoning him toward her with her left arm, her right index finger held up to her lips, requesting silence.

Much like at the marine center, as he got closer to the tank the buzzing sound he'd been hearing shifted to a garbled mix of tones, this time similar to the cocktail parties his mom hosted at the house. The dolphins' squeaks became more pronounced as he inched closer on his hands and knees. They seemed to almost be talking to each other.

"Sit here," whispered Taylor, pointing to a spot right next to her.

Noah pushed his back up against the cool side of the tank and looked at his friend.

"Now what?" she asked.

Noah looked behind him at the tank, and was startled to see the two dolphins' heads staring silently at him from the water. "Okay, that's weird."

As if in response, the two dolphins let out a series of chatters, like they were laughing at him.

From the far side of the enclosed area, Noah could make out the barks of the harbor seals, as if they were chiming in.

Each bark sounded like an echo in Noah's mind and emitted a flash of an image, like their vocal intonations controlled an internal slide show. As he took a deep breath and slowly let it out, he willed away the buzzing, pushing it deep into his subconscious.

Unlike before, when he tried to catch everything being said and see every image flying through his mind, Noah tried to free his mind of any thought and allow the images to come freely.

Taylor watched him in amazement. "Are they talking to you?" she asked, trying to mask the sense that she was witnessing something no one ever has before. "Can you hear what they're trying to say?"

"I don't think I'm hearing their words," said Noah. "I think I'm seeing them. And what I'm seeing is scaring the crap out of me."

24.

The glass containers clinked loudly inside the large plastic tub as Jake heaved it onto the metal desktop. He opened the lid and peered inside, then carefully began to remove the specimen jars he brought from the boat. He had to move quickly. He knew Taylor had been in the office, but he didn't know how much information had been compromised about the Trident project.

He looked at the phone, wondering what was taking the security guards so long.

The first jar held murky water pulled from the ocean depths. Jake lifted the liquid-filled container, swirling it and then allowing dense particles to settle at the bottom. Opening a drawer to the right, he pulled out a handful of syringes and placed them on the cool metal surface. The top of each jar had a rubber stopper with a deep hole in its center so he could pull liquid out without upsetting the jar's contents.

While holding the jar steady with his left hand, Jake carefully inserted the first syringe, extracting the murky brown liquid from the uppermost part of the container. Setting the jar aside, he pulled a microscope slide from the second drawer and carefully dropped the liquid in the center of the rectangular piece of glass. Placing another slide on top, he sat on a black swivel chair and rolled himself to a bank of microscopes flanking the opposing wall.

He slipped the slide in and peered through the lens, slowly adjusting the focus, turning the knob on the side. "I'll be damned," he said softly. He jotted notes meticulously in a manila file folder marked "Field Reports" as he continued the process with each of the jars.

The last jar held a gelatinous mass about the size of an apricot. Its spotted green surface was dimpled, the edges sliced cleanly as if by a razor. Jake held the jar up to the light, observing how the piece of flesh reflected points of light. It seemed almost luminescent. He lifted the cap off the jar, and slowly pulled a piece of the flesh away using large tweezers, then dropped it between two three-inch rectangular pieces of glass and rolled himself back to the microscope. The only sound in the room was the soft click of the large clock hung above the door. Jake held his breath as he brought the slide into focus, then exhaled with a single word of triumph: "Incredible."

25.

Taylor looked closely at Noah for any hint that he might be messing with her. They leaned against a chain link fence near the dolphin tanks, the mammals' high-pitched whines and clicks echoing in the air above the water. Noah stared off into the distance, his pale eyes blank, his face slack.

"What are you seeing that's scary?" she whispered.

"It's like the home movies of the dark and sinister," Noah said slowly, each word coming out in monotone. "I see water, deep water. Then it clicks. I see jagged teeth . . . they're coming fast. Then it's gone. Red. Blood. An anchor plunging into the water, I think. It's fast."

The two dolphins let out a whistle, and Noah clapped his hands over his ears, his eyes shut tight. "Noah?" Taylor grabbed his shoulders. "Noah, what's wrong?"

"It's too fast, too much," he said through gritted teeth. "It hurts to watch; the images are flying by me. I feel like I'm stuck on some crazy carousel, out of control."

The dolphins began to chatter between each other with clicks, whines and whistles. "What are they saying?" she asked.

"It's not like they're speaking English," Noah said, rubbing a blooming headache away from his temples. "It's like they talk in pure emotion. I'm just filled with different feelings; it's like they can manipulate how I'm feeling. It's intense." Noah clenched his fists, fighting to control a sense of impending doom and a desire to run.

He looked at the dolphins in the tank. "What are you trying to tell me?" He disregarded Taylor's penetrating stare. The desire to run nearly overtook him, and Noah felt like his skin was crawling, like he needed to run now.

The two dolphins leapt from the water and came crashing down on their backs. The water flew, splashing on the deck and covering Noah. He could taste the salt as he licked his lips, but it wasn't particularly pleasant. There was an unnatural aspect to it. He spat onto the deck as he whisked water off his arms.

"Something's wrong, but I don't know what it is. I just think we have to get out of here. I don't think it's safe," Noah said to Taylor. "I'm feeling like I'm staring down the headlights of an oncoming train. Like if we don't move, we'll be crushed. All this emotion is slamming into me." He began rubbing at his temples with the heels of his palms. "It's like I felt with the whales. But this time it's different. And the images are really gross."

"Is it like scientific gross or horror movie gross?" Taylor asked.

"It's some freakish thing with jagged teeth. And big eyes," Noah said in a monotone whisper. Sweat broke out on his forehead, and he slowly wiped it away, almost in a trance.

"Where'd they see it?"

"I don't know. Looks like open water. Not a tank," Noah said, his brow furrowing. "The images are too fast." He looked over at the dolphin tank, and the two dolphins popped their heads up above the water's surface, staring at him. The larger dolphin on the left nodded its head, making three clicking sounds.

Four images flashed: the murky ocean; the three-pronged anchor; the teeth rushing; a crimson fog spreading its tendrils in the depths of the undulating sea.

One word popped into his mind: *Run*.

Taylor pulled the pages from her backpack, and flipped through text, noting the intricate drawings of underwater plants and sea life dotting each page, reading the observations. Noah knew she was recording the pages in her mind; he had always envied the way she could remember everything she saw in detail.

Toward the middle of the stack, she found the drawing of a large oblong creature that took up the entire page, flippers ending in long serrated claws, its mouth a tangle of jagged teeth, large eyes menacing. Along the side of the sketch were tiny notes and lines showing estimates of recent growth. It was hand drawn and someone had scanned it into the computer.

"Noah . . . look at this," Taylor said, offering the page to her friend, pointing at the picture and the note beneath it.

Under the sketch, one sentence was written: *Released, October 15, 2015.*

"That was three months ago."

***

The office in the lab was dark except for one pinprick of light shining on a specimen jar, its contents suspended. The section of dark green flesh floated like soft feathers in the clear liquid.

Jake jostled the contents again slightly with his left hand, holding the jar at eye level, looking for any discoloration that might point to the cause for the thickened skin. He jotted notes meticulously in a file opened on the shiny metal table surface. Putting down the jar, he flipped another page, leaning forward as he made more tiny notations.

Walking his wheeled chair back over to the credenza, he noticed the computer screen was on. He was sure it was off when they left. He quickly typed in the password. The files were still there, documents detailing the work that had taken over his life. Still, an uneasiness settled over him. He would need to move the information to a more secure location.

The phone rang harshly, startling Jake from his thoughts. He barked into the receiver. "Did you find them?"

"Find who?" a high-pitched voice said on the other end.

"Sorry, I thought you were someone else."

"This wasn't what I agreed to," the voice continued. "This has gone way too far, much farther than we first discussed. We need to stop."

"That's not an option," Jake said sternly. "The project has built momentum over the years; it was bound to change course in some areas. You know that. You knew what risks we were taking when I asked for your involvement, and you did nothing then. You understood there could be consequences, a few setbacks—"

"Setbacks?" the voice screamed on the other end. "How can you be so cavalier about something that could affect the entire ecosystem? This is not just a blip in the data. We're not talking about a simple anomaly at the laboratory. This is not the direction I thought it would take!"

Jake hissed for woman to be quiet. "No, it may not be, but you misunderstand. This is not your decision to make. This is no longer our project; it's mine. My findings and work will change the complexity of the world. It's not time to back down." He waited for another screaming session, and was surprised with the cool response.

"You took it too far," she said. "We never set out to change the course of human genetics, and certainly not to destroy more of what we were setting out to save. This needs to be contained."

"I'm taking care of it." Then he hung up the phone.

***

Jake was just turning out the lights of the office when the detective from the beach earlier that day arrived.

"Do you have a second, Dr. Stafford?"

"Actually, I was just heading out."

Ignoring him, the detective pushed past Jake, adding, "This won't take long. Is Dr. Borcelli around? I'd like to include her in this discussion."

"She's not here," Jake said coolly. "Won't be back for a while."

"That's a shame. She seemed the most intrigued by the claw we found in the victim and I was hoping to get a bit more information."

Jake looked at the clock.

"Like I said, I'm not sure what that was, but I had never seen anything like it."

"We were hoping you could determine its origin. The species, based on its DNA, correct? You are a geneticist, right?"

"Yes, that's right." Jake took another quick glance at the clock. "If you can leave the specimen with us, we'd be happy to look into it."

The detective shifted uncomfortably. "Well, that's just the thing," he said. "I gave the specimen to Dr. Borcelli at the beach." Seconds passed in silence. "You haven't seen it?"

"No, sorry." Jake flipped on the lights and waved his arm around the room, pointing toward the specimen jars. "You're welcome to look."

"That's okay. I'll just wait until Dr. Borcelli returns."

"It could be a while," Jake said. "She went out on a dive."

"How long do those usually take?"

"Hours. Sometimes days," Jake said, thinking: Sometimes an eternity.

The detective handed Jake his card. "Just call me when she gets in, will you? We'd like to get this taken care of as quickly as possible. Your help is much appreciated."

The phone began to ring, but Jake ignored it, instead giving the detective a mock salute with the card, dimples deepening with his smile. "Don't worry. I'll take care of everything."

26.

Taylor sat crouched against the dolphin tank and flipped through the pages, digesting information as she went. "Did you know she was working on a project that involved some kind of genetic engineering?"

"What are you talking about?" Noah said to the floor, his palms smashed against his forehead.

"Here," Taylor said. "Take a look at this. There are diagrams in here . . . about this thing she drew, like measurements and stuff." Taylor flipped a few pages ahead. "Here! Look at the way she noted changes in development, and there are several seals listed here right next to the 'thing.'"

Noah leaned over to look at the page. "Looks like she was just tracking their growth."

"But it's more than just regular stuff like flipper length, and how many teeth. She calls them fangs here. Look at this line: skin abnormalities. And this one: luminescence?" Taylor began flipping through the pages more quickly, and stopped near the last part of the pages containing a chart. "And check this out. She's listed months of research here. Response to external vocal stimuli," Taylor read.

"What's that have to do with genetic engineering?"

"I think my mom was doing some crazy stuff, Noah, and I think we were part of it. Your name's on this chart, Noah. She was documenting your behavior."

"What—like I was some kind of research specimen?"

"She seemed to be interested in your ability to stay under water."

"I only did it that one time at the pool."

"It looks like it might have happened more than that time. Look." Taylor flipped through several pages of notes, stopping on one page filled with a chart listing dates. "'December 18, 2003,'" Taylor read, "'Noah is showing unique behaviors. Today, he slipped underwater while bathing and his mother thought he had drowned. She said he was an inch below the surface, staring up at her when she came into the bathroom. She screamed and he stood up in the tub as if nothing had happened.'"

"I don't remember that."

"You were two years old, Noah."

Taylor scanned the chart further. "Listen to this. 'September 1, 2004 . . . experiment involving forty gallon barrel filled with water, kids bobbing for apples at Taylor's third birthday party, Noah stayed under the water for thirty seconds, and emerged with an apple in his mouth. He showed no signs of discomfort or oxygen deprivation.'"

"My mom would have freaked out," Noah said.

"Maybe she wasn't there. I had a bunch of parties that she just dropped you off, remember? When she had that art class she taught on the weekends? The way these charts look, I think my mom might have been putting you in quite a few situations here. Testing you . . . Here's that day when you were at the pool with your mom. Look. 'Today's events seem to confirm the characteristics believed connected with the genetic transformation.'"

"I always knew I was a freak," mumbled Noah as he looked at his webbed fingers.

"Noah . . . this is amazing! If what my mom's notes say is right, then you have a gift. What if you can swim like the seals? What if you can communicate with them or these dolphins," she said, pointing to the bobbing grey heads staring at them. She started to laugh. "Check them out! They look like they understand what I'm saying. Can you hear what they're thinking?"

"They think you're nuts," Noah said flatly.

"Maybe the images are how they talk. Maybe you're just plugged into it . . . you can do it, like they do. If what's happening to you is a genetic mutation, so what? Every one of us is constantly mutating, evolving based on circumstances, don't you think? When I was a girl, I would spend hours at the tide pools and I knew every one of the species we saw. It was really amazing. Creatures that once inhabited the ocean depths had learned to adapt to little or no water during part of the day. How is this different?"

"Uh . . . I don't live in a tide pool?"

"You know what I mean, Noah."

The two dolphins dropped below the surface, and began circling in the tank, their tails agitating the water to the point that it began to spill over the sides. Noah thought about all the times Taylor's mom would smile at him, her soft emerald eyes crinkled at the edges as she ruffled his hair. He'd known her so long, he thought of her as family. Now he realized he probably spent a lot more time with her than he remembered—as a specimen.

Even at the young age of five, Noah knew the minute details about hundreds of marine creatures. He would beg his mom to go to the aquarium in Monterey to see the otters and harbor seals, and he would stand for hours, hands dug deep inside his pockets as he walked to each separate tank and quietly cataloged everything he knew.

For a while, they seemed to visit aquariums almost every weekend. It was the one thing his mom knew they could do that could make Noah smile non-stop. Kate was always with them, Taylor in tow. He wondered if his own mom knew he was part of an experiment.

Taylor inched closer to Noah, feeling more uncomfortable since the dolphins continued to bob in the same spot, unwavering, looking intently at the two teens.

"You know how I said I'm seeing pictures in my head?"

Taylor nodded.

"Well, I don't think it's as important to see what the images are; I think it's more important to understand what the images represent, and how that makes me feel. It's like sending an emotion I need to feel, and then I act on the emotion."

Noah looked at the dolphins, and they both chirped in response. An image flashed of a baby smiling. Be happy. *Are they trying to comfort me?* That was the most confusing thing about the images. It was kind of a crapshoot. Noah was going to have to trust his gut about what they were trying to tell him, but he had spent a large part of his childhood squashing his intuition. He blew out a deep breath, trying hard to concentrate. A new aroma swirled in the air, like a musky deodorant.

A tingling sensation rose from deep in his abdomen, and the dolphins became more agitated. "Something's wrong," he said.

A heavy metal door slammed with a clang from the far end of the hallway, and a rumble of men's voices bounced off the walls. The buzzing returned, a deafening roar in Noah's ears. Noah looked over at the tank. The two dolphins swam inches apart in tight circles, increasing their chatter with each passing as if a tether was vaulting them around.

They let out a large chirp that echoed off the walls and leapt from the water before landing hard on their sides. Images flashed in Noah's mind: children running, babies crawling. Intuitively, he knew what they were trying to say: *flee.*

As a wall of water hit Taylor and Noah, the dolphins darted together toward the back, intent on repeating the process. Another tank across some wooden decking was covered with tarps. One harbor seal and two California sea lions began barking as if cheering the dolphins on. Noah could hear water thrashing as they cried out.

"Noah, what's happening?"

One of the dolphins used its tail to vault water over the tank while the other leapt in circles, clearly upset. The cries from the covered tank became frantic. The voices from the hallway became louder, the footfalls rushing toward them. Images flashed in Noah's mind, and he pushed the buzzing noise down until it merely sounded like a light hiss. The images came in quick succession: A small dog running in fear; a mountain lion chasing a rabbit; a squirrel rushing up a tree trunk. *Flee, flee, flee.*

The dolphins took another synchronized leap and Taylor screamed, thinking they were going to leap from the tank.

"We have to get out of here, Tay. To the beach, the water."

Noah pulled her arm and took off running, jumping a wooden railing that walled off the bluffs facing the ocean and led to the private beach below. As they ran, Noah could hear a seal barking in the distance.

"What's happening?" Taylor screamed.

"Just run!"

***

Jake was shredding documents when the phone began to ring again. He picked it up quickly, ready to continue the argument, but was surprised to hear it was one of the security guards. "Kids were in the dolphin tanks, sir. They ran off toward the bluffs."

"Dr. Borcelli's daughter?" Jake asked.

"Yeah, and her friend, the kid with the deformed hands. The dolphins are pretty shook up. There's water everywhere. I'm not sure what they were doing with them or how they got in here. Should we go after them, sir?"

"Yeah, they can't get far. Once you find them, bring them back to the dolphin tanks. I have a few questions to ask them. I'm on my way."

"Will you tell Dr. Borcelli?"

"Of course. I'll take care of everything."

Jake lightly dropped the receiver back into its cradle and returned to his research, shaking his head slowly, a soft chuckle bubbling from his chest as he once again squinted into the ocular lens. He jotted a few notes in the manila folder next to him, closed the file and returned it to the locked file cabinet.

Now the fun really begins.

***

Detective Gomez's large boots marked off a loud cadence, echoing off the floating boats and skimmers surrounding the dock as he made his way down the wooden slats toward the marina office. Zeke answered quickly, disengaging the deadbolt and pulling the detective inside.

"What is it now, Zeke?"

The marina owner almost seemed to shake in the waning indoor light. He looked past the detective, as if the door would spring open, releasing a world of monsters intent on killing him. "Thanks for coming out so quick," Zeke said, his head bobbing in supplication as he eyed the closed door behind the detective.

"You said it was urgent." Detective Gomez looked around the small office, expecting to see a body on the ground or the place ransacked. "So? What's up?"

"I want to report a missing person."

Gomez grabbed a small notebook from his front pocket and clicked open a pen. "Go ahead."

"She was on the boat, but didn't come back," Zeke said.

"Whose boat?"

"Jake Stafford's."

Detective Gomez took a cleansing breath, trying his best to keep a professional appearance. "Who are we talking about?"

"Pretty gal. Brownish hair, green eyes. Bitty thing." Zeke rubbed his neck with a dirty rag and continued to shoot glances at the heavy door behind the detective. "I don't know her name, but she's been on his boat before."

"If she was missing, why didn't Dr. Stafford report something? I just saw him, Zeke."

"He went out with her, and she wasn't on the boat when he came back."

"Zeke, are you sure you just didn't miss seeing her? Have you been watching the boat all this time?"

"Don't need to," he said. He opened the door of the marina office and pointed up to one of the eaves of the roof. "I got a special camera pointed just at him. Watch him all the time."

27.

Noah ran along the small trail that meandered through scrub and lavender, and he nearly tripped as he glanced at the ocean.

Ten seals jumped out of the water in unison, mimicking the dolphins' behavior, leaping then crashing into the white foam spread out on the crest of a wave. In all the years he'd been watching marine mammals in the wild, Noah had never seen that type of behavior with seals. They'd jump from the water occasionally, but they usually would leap tightly into an oncoming wave or simply poked their heads up to break the surface. To see all of them fly straight up and splash down in unison was weird.

It was like something he'd see in a show at Sea World. Choreographed, rehearsed.

Images flashed in his mind: darting seals in a sea of bubbles; the seal they had found on the beach, gashes freshly oozing; a threatening slash of razor sharp teeth.

Noah figured out a way to compartmentalize the images so they didn't drive him crazy; he could focus on other things while they happened—kind of like secretly checking a text while talking to his mom at dinnertime.

He realized what the images were saying, what emotion they were expressing: fear.

But fear of what?

Noah was having trouble navigating the sandy path in the late afternoon light. The sun cast strange shadows on the shore. The sky was filled with dark gray storm clouds, shafts of light piercing through, creating an ambient glow reflecting on the water. The sand was deep, wet and cool when they hit the beach. Noah struggled to keep his footing; his flip-flops dug into the soft surface and slipped as the moist sand accumulated on the bottom of the rubber soles.

When he reached the water's edge, he had an uncontrollable urge to keep running, but Taylor stopped him, grabbing him by the shirt and dragging him toward a dark cave entrance carved about five feet high into the cliff face.

"This way!" she yelled.

The inside of the cave was damp and musty, the pungent scent of seawater intermingling with the loam from the slimy rock surface. Each step made a soft gushing sound as they pushed into the enclosure. Their breath made a raspy echo as they pushed farther inside.

Once near the back, Taylor dropped down, her knees creating small divots the size of half-shelled coconuts in the soft ground. She turned toward Noah, wiping her hands on her jeans.

"Now what?" Noah examined the shiny walls of the cave, feeling along the smooth surface. "Seems we're kind of stuck in here. Is there another way out?"

"Nope."

Noah looked at Taylor with a mixture of annoyance and incredulity. "Then why'd you bring me in here! I was close to—"

"Close to what, Noah?" Taylor whispered, crossing her arms defiantly. "You were going in there, weren't you? You can't swim, remember?"

"I think I—"

"Listen, I know you're going through a lot. But I had to stop you. We're safe here, for now."

"What do you mean 'for now'?"

"We just wait, stay quiet, and once they move on to search near the birds of prey, we'll head back to the lab."

"But . . ."

"Wait." Taylor listened intently. "I think I hear something."

Noah could hear it, too. Muffled voices. Although he knew it was probably the security guards looking for them, he was relieved that the voices weren't coming from inside his head. He was learning to recognize the difference between regular human voices and the buzzing intonations, which seemed to come in waves. The voices they were hearing now were definitely masculine, and Noah could tell they were close.

"Did you check the cave?" one voice said.

"I'm not going in there," another said. "That's where the mountain lion was spotted." Noah and Taylor shared a look, then shifted their gaze into the cave's darkened depths.

"Just check it," the first voice said, annoyed.

A beam of light illuminated the far wall across from Taylor and began a slow sweep around. Taylor pulled her feet up against her legs and they both squished themselves against the wall.

Noah leaned over and whispered in Taylor's ear: "Our footprints."

"I ran up the bluff and around the hill before I yanked you in here," she whispered back, her breath tickling the small hairs on Noah's ears.

She put her finger to her lips. The flashlight did one more sweep before blinking off.

They still heard the man's voice, but it was receding. "I think they're going," Noah whispered. Taylor nodded, motioning them to sit tight.

As the seconds ticked away, a renewed sense of unease grew as Noah thought about what the first guard had said. The cave walls seemed to be closing around them. Electric shockwaves coursed through Noah with each muffled sound that echoed within the cave.

Taylor motioned for Noah to follow her as she began to crawl out on her stomach.

"What are you doing?" he hissed.

"It'll be good to stay close to the ground in case they're out there," she whispered. "They'll be standing up, so probably won't be looking down. We can peek out without being seen as easily."

Tiny pebbles and sand dug into Noah's elbows and sand spilled over into the top of his shorts. Grains of shale took tiny round bites from his knees as he slithered behind Taylor toward the cave entrance. Noah could see the ocean in the distance. He knew he should be looking for any sign of the security guards, but he couldn't help searching the water for any sign of the seals they saw earlier.

"Come on." Taylor said. "I think the coast is clear."

She stood up and dusted off her knees, careful to keep an eye out for anyone coming along the trail, then started inching her way around the side of the cliff face toward the bluff.

"Where are you going?" Noah whispered harshly as he moved his torso side to side. Taylor simply responded by turning her head and bringing her finger to her lips.

Staying close to the outside of the cave, Taylor pushed her back against the wet rock black-ops-style, inching closer to the trailhead. Noah took a minute to push himself onto his knees and brush off the grit embedded in his elbow skin.

When he turned around to tell Taylor to wait, he saw her standing ramrod straight, staring at the darkening bunches of scrub brush scattered along the hillside.

Then Noah heard the mountain lion's low growl. The large cat was perched on the bluff in the distance, its head low, every muscle tensed.

Noah could see Taylor's chest rising and falling, could sense the fear coursing through her body as she began to inch back toward the cave entrance.

"Just hold still," Noah hissed, his eyes cutting between her trembling body and the crouching cat. "I'll create a diversion. Head to the lab. Get help. Get Dr. Stafford."

Noah stood to his full height, bringing the gaze of the cat's shining yellow eyes to him.

Something within him changed: A sense of calm radiated through him. His vision seemed sharper.

"Come and get me," he whispered. Then he began waving his arms as he ran.

"No, Noah!" Taylor screamed. "Don't run!"

Everything seemed to happen in a split-second. The cat's muscular body was a blur, blending with the scrub brush and the sandy ground below as it charged at Noah running toward the surf.

28.

Taylor reached the edge of the trailhead and turned around to see Noah rush into the water and dive through one of the wakes, disappearing behind a wall of white foam. She picked up a stone the size of a baby tortoise and with a sideways pitch, flung it at the cat. She got lucky; the rock struck its left flank, sending the cat crashing through the shallow waves just a few feet from where Noah had disappeared.

Taylor quickly backed up and grabbed for a large stick, readying herself for a fight, but the cat ran off toward the bluff, crisscrossing its way through the tufts of scrub and berry dotting the shoreline.

Still holding her weapon, feet spread wide, knees bent ready for an attack, Taylor scanned the surf, taking deep gulping breaths as she searched for her friend's head to break the surface of the shimmering water.

"Noah!" she called. "Are you okay?"

She felt a flood of relief when a dark head popped up on the crest of a wave fifty yards away. "Noah! Thank God," she said as she took a few steps toward the water.

Two other dark heads popped to the surface just inches from the first, the last sounding off in a friendly bark.

"Sea lions," she said, still recovering her breath and scanning the horizon for any sign of her friend. The wind intensified, carrying her scream across the rolling waves.

"Noah! Where are you?"

Another sea lion barked its response before the three heads disappeared under the water.

Her friend was gone.

***

Noah was surprised how warm the water seemed as he lunged forward, his knees punching through the ocean foam as he ran. The sea floor sucked hungrily at his flip-flops, finally loosening them from his feet as he dove into the water. Each hand was cupped, loose fingers extending his webbing as he frantically pushing through the incoming waves.

As he dove in, arching his body gracefully, cutting into the dark water, his mind focused on one thing: escape. His muscles strained with each pull forward, his mind racing as his legs did quick scissor kicks behind him. Those few lessons from when he was a kid seemed to spring forward from the depths of his mind.

Just before he disappeared into the surf, Noah heard the splashing of the large cat's paws behind him; its high-pitched growl sent shockwaves of fear coursing down his spine.

Noah broke through the first waves and was under water, swimming effortlessly, each stroke igniting a sense of wonder and excitement as his swift kicks propelling him out to sea. The skin between his misshapen fingers ballooned like small cups capturing the water and forcing it behind him.

He was surprised at how easily he glided; it almost felt like he was flying. He forgot all about the mountain lion as his eyes adjusted to this strange underwater world. He was surprised that he could see anything. And the water didn't sting his eyes; it didn't even seem murky.

Noah marveled at how beautiful the ocean was at dusk.

As he swam farther from shore, Noah's lungs began a slow burn, but he didn't want to chance coming to the surface and facing the claws and sharp teeth of his pursuer. He pushed himself deeper under the swaying water, fighting the urge to breath, forcing himself into a calming state.

The slow burn in his lungs began to fade and he kicked harder to extend the distance from shore.

Giddy with this newfound ability, he swirled in a corkscrew motion. He shifted his body in a quick arc and took one last look behind him.

No mountain lion.

He was safe.

As he turned to kick off toward shore, three large California sea lions darted past him, sending swirls of tiny bubbles in their wake. Five feet away, deeper in the dark gray water, he began to see the outline of a fourth sea lion charging toward him, mouth agape. Noah's heart raced, his thoughts frantic and he considered how to escape, but nothing sprang to mind.

All Noah could do was watch as the large brown creature's maw gently closed around his right ankle and began to pull him deeper and farther out to sea.

A stream of oblong bubbles floating upward behind him was the only evidence that Noah had ever been there.

29.

Taylor fell to her knees, the stick dropping weakly from her grasp as she screamed Noah's name over an intensifying blast of wind. She scanned the horizon, searching every incoming wave for any sign of her friend, but there was nothing.

Dread weighed her down, the panic overtaking her mind and paralyzing her limbs. She turned to see Doc Stafford lurching forward along the path, the wind spraying fine loose gravel against his unshaven face.

She uttered a barely audible plea, whispering, "Help me. . . . Noah."

She couldn't move, her knees firmly planted in the wet sand, her body heavy with the totality of what she thought was happening. Her friend was gone.

A numbness settled in and Taylor let the wind attack her body, welcoming the ferocity of it. She could see Doc Stafford running toward her through the whipping curtain of her tangled hair. His hands tightly gripped her shoulders, but his voice seemed miles away.

"Where's the boy?" he screamed.

She feebly pointed her index finger at the ocean, a tear tracking down her right cheek. "He's . . . he . . ."

"Taylor!" Jake gave her shoulders a small shake. "What happened? Where's Noah?"

"It's . . . he . . . mountain lion," Taylor mumbled.

Jake knew about the cat. For the past month, the security guards at the lab had been tracking one in the bluffs, mainly because they didn't want it to get into the area where they keep the birds of prey. Most mountain lions scare off fairly easily when they encounter humans, but this one recently charged two researchers and had nearly killed a small dog being walked off leash on a trail nearby.

They had called the sheriff's office out and local wildlife experts set traps, but the cat had been elusive. Although they posted signs at the marine center and advised the docents to be alert for any signs of the cat, there were no other sightings.

Until now.

"Where is he?" Jake asked more forcefully. He looked around the beach, thinking Noah might be hurt nearby.

Taylor's shaky finger continued to point out to sea. "There," she whispered. "He's out there."

Jake ran into the incoming waves, searching the sandy bottom with his hands, screaming Noah's name as he crisscrossed deeper into the ocean, frantic to find the body in time to start CPR.

Taylor watched in numb silence, unable to move, unable to comprehend what had just happened.

30.

The voice seemed to come from the end of a dark far-away tunnel; Noah wondered if it was real or if he was in a dream. Images flashed in his mind: bubbles floating to the surface; a boy's chest expanding; gusts of wind skimming across the water.

Breathe, he thought.

He wondered if he was dead. He was in the ocean, but he was warm, content. That didn't seem right. And he was aware that he was moving, being pulled by something. His right ankle ached and he looked down to see it still secure inside a large brown mouth. He was surrounded by an inky black darkness, pops and gurgles of the underwater world accompanying him on his descent.

Noah sensed movement on his skin, a ripple of water against his cheeks as his hair danced behind him. The pressure in his chest was like a vice, but the buzzing that had filled his head was gone.

Images continued to spring into his mind: a sunset; the stillness of the water; sunshine sparkling like diamonds on the ocean surface.

Peaceful, Noah thought.

The images helped loosen his chest, relax his mind.

Everything seemed to move so slowly, but he felt good. Better than he had felt in a long time. He felt like he was floating on a cloud. From above he began to see small shafts of light cutting into the water's surface and new images rushed in: the cave; the mountain lion; the gaping maw of a sea lion.

Was he seeing his life flash before him?

I must be dying, he thought.

Noah looked up, more curious than afraid. Bright shafts of light seemed to spin and then to retreat from his vision. He had heard stories about surfers who had been pulled under the waves and how they had seen a tunnel of light appear and a weightlessness before they found themselves coughing up sea water on the beach, a lifeguard's face just inches from their own.

Was this what they were talking about? Nearly dead. Angels. Harps. White light. Curtains.

He thought about his mom and his heart ached.

As he began to close his eyes in submission, the whiskered face of a sea lion rose gently next to him, its large brown eyes filled with curiosity. It made a soft bark, causing a bubble of air to escape from its jaws. Noah heard it again, much louder this time, more like a belch. The word "peace" reverberated in Noah's head. He wondered if the seal would raise its flipper to extend two fingers in a sign of solidarity.

He grinned, blinking his response, surprised that he wasn't scared, the desperation for oxygen to fill his lungs had dissipated.

I won't get more peaceful than this, he thought. I'm dead, right?

The seal's mouth opened wider, seeming to break into a smile. It barked out something, causing another bubble of air to begin rising toward the surface. Noah watched it float away, mesmerized by its beauty.

Images clicked through Noah's mind: seals swimming in a line; fish following one another on the ocean floor. Seconds later, a voice boomed inside Noah's head.

"Come."

Startled, Noah tried to push away, but his ankle erupted in pain. A cold rush of salt water filled his lungs, clamping his chest tight as if being crushed in the strong grip of a wrestler. As his arms spun frantically, Noah kicked off hard, dislodging the soft jaws of the sea lion that held his ankle gently from below.

As he kicked toward the surface, he knew he wouldn't make it. He was too deep. He looked around him, realizing the water seemed incredibly clear although he knew that the afternoon sun was low and it would be dark soon.

Light danced off the bulbs of seaweed that swayed in the ocean depths.

Tiny dots of flotsam passed by him in swirls as seven seals circled around him, occasionally stopping their water dance to look closely at his face and bob their heads knowingly before speeding off in a swirl of bubbles. They continued this curious underwater dance until Noah calmed down. He realized the water he'd taken in wasn't causing his chest to explode or his body to succumb to its effects.

His mind reeled in confusion. This is so weird, he thought. Then he tried to convince himself that it wasn't such a bad way to go. Could be worse: I could be in the jaws of the mountain lion.

Noah slowly pushed water up and down with his fanned hands, now resigned to this last goodbye before inhaling another blast of water. Warmth settled deep within him and he waited for consciousness to slip away. As he floated, waiting, three seals lined up just a foot from the tip of his nose, staring intently at him and twisting their faces left and right in bemused silence.

The largest of the three harbor seals belch-barked, a bubble of air escaping to the surface. Simultaneously, a deep voice croaked in his mind.

"Come."

The three flipped their tail fins and sped off into the darkness, leaving him all alone watching the swirl of bubbles in their wake.

Still treading water fifty feet below the surface, Noah looked up. The soft shafts of light cascaded down before being blotted by something swimming above him.

A harbor seal rose silently from below, its eyes imploring; it began to push against Noah's side with its head. It didn't take a brain surgeon to know what the creature was trying to tell him. "Move."

Noah saw the seal's jaw open and close before it sped off, its muscular body catapulting it through the darkening water in the distance.

The same voice he now recognized as the voice of these creatures boomed within him: "Flee."

***

As the deep hues of the ocean enveloped the quiet rhythm of the waning afternoon, Bessy continued to circle from below, constantly aware of her surroundings and the echoes of other marine life settling into the impending night.

She knew the others wavered just feet below the surface, but she waited. Her large body stopped and peered upward periodically to listen for any sign of movement on the surface, bobbing easily, using misshapen flippers to keep herself steadily in one location before sliding silently forward again, faint afternoon light casting strange shadows on her mottled skin.

Nearly equal to the size of many small pleasure boats that cruised the waterways on sunny afternoons, Bessy could cut through the water with speed and agility. As her predatory instincts improved, she was no longer satiated by the small waterfowl and fish found near the coastline, and she had begun to dive deeper looking for larger prey but the pressure of the water's depths sharply sliced into her skull making each dive a painful experience.

While hunger urged her forward, a remaining glimmer of intelligent thought held her back; the strange creature vaguely remembered the fear and pain she had felt in the tanks at the lab.

The memory of the tapping on the side of the boat followed by the scrape along its hull was unmistakable. Images of a smiling face and feelings of safety and love flooded the creature's mind before shifting, then slowly unraveling into one searing thought:

Kill.

31.

Jake sat down hard, punching his fist at the incoming waves. Taylor looked on in stunned silence. "We need to get help," he said. "Get a boat and get out there."

"He can't swim," Taylor said feebly.

"There's still time."

"How? How is there time?" Taylor screamed. "He's been out there underwater for too long!"

"He was changing. It was working," Jake said, almost to himself.

"What are you talking about?"

"We were so close. I just needed to—" Jake pushed his hands through his hair, thinking. "We need to go get him. Come on. There's a Zodiac in the research hanger off the estuary. I'll need your help."

Taylor looked up at Jake with a combination of confusion and anger. "We're going out there on a boat? We should call 911, or something. Get search and rescue involved."

"Not going to happen. Time's wasting."

"Where's my mom? She'll know what to do."

"She's out there; on a dive." Jake grabbed Taylor's arm, pulling her up. "We have to go. Now."

"He can't swim. He—"

Jake grabbed Taylor's shoulders lightly and looked deeply into her eyes. "You'll have to trust me, Taylor. He's part of something big . . . bigger than you can imagine. And he'll be fine, if we find him right now."

"My mom's project, right?" Taylor whispered. "The Trident Initiative?"

A flash of irritation washed across Jake's brow, but he forced a smile. "Yeah, right. Your mom's project."

"I saw his name . . ."

"She released something . . . something dangerous."

"Bessy?"

"She's not sweet Bessy anymore, Taylor. And the kid's out there with it. We have to get Noah before it does."

Jake pulled her away from the shoreline, leading her toward a small waterway near the cave, and a large building housing research equipment nearby.

Taylor looked behind her at the vast ocean, the waves crashing against the rocky cliffs. "How will we find him? The ocean's huge."

"His mom put a GPS tracking chip under his skin when he was little."

"How do you know that?"

"Your mom told me."

Taylor stumbled as Jake pulled her along. "Aren't those chips a bit unethical?" she asked.

Jake laughed at that. "Whether it's unethical or not is immaterial; right now, it's going to help us find your friend."

***

At first, Noah thought he was losing consciousness when he started to see the dancing lights in the water. He could barely discern the outline of the sea lion as it retreated in the distance, but the water around him seemed to come to life.

He felt like he was immersed in a mystical mixture of colors like the northern skies of Nova Scotia. A fine mist of aqua blue and streaks of purple and orange danced in arcs, creating a path of iridescent watercolor leading the way.

The pounding in Noah's head subsided and he regained a sense of calm as he kicked off toward the retreating bubbles. Like he did when swimming in the community pool, Noah focused on his strokes and kicks, but there was an effortlessness about it now.

He was completely lost in the moment, and he wondered how he could have ever missed out on this experience before. His promise to his mom had kept him on the surface for so long, but in the deep water, it was completely different.

It's like I'm in a dream, he thought. It doesn't feel real.

With each stroke, he gained a sense of power, his fingers splayed to their limits, the skin between each finger ballooning with the weight of the water, yet he felt no discomfort. The movement required no thought. Each push of his hands toward his sides was done in perfect unison, much like the sea creatures he'd watched with such awe at the aquarium or on TV.

He kicked off and spun his body, mimicking the actions of the sea lion ahead of him. His chest no longer tight, his mind clear from all thought as his body closed the gap between the sea lion and himself.

Noah let out a bubble of air, mentally calling for the animal to wait.

He was excited to see the creature turn its body in a tight arc and float gently in the soft blue water ahead. As he swam up to the large brown creature, Noah noticed a deep gash in the sea lion's head, extending several inches from its right eye to its neck. Noah reached out to touch it, but the sea lion twisted away, continuing its retreat before looking back at Noah, expecting him to follow.

I know . . . you don't have to tell me again, Noah thought.

It did anyway.

"Come."

***

The underwater world gurgled with life as Noah followed the animal swiftly retreating into the darkness. He assumed it had been about ten minutes since he took his last breath of air and he marveled at how he was still alive. *Maybe this is heaven*, he thought as he kicked hard with his bare feet.

Each stroke of his arms became more fluid as he pushed through the cold water, but Noah no longer felt the spiky chill that had permeated his skin. He now felt a soft comforting glow around his entire body.

It felt like the times when he fell asleep on the beach when there was a hint of a breeze, the sun caressing every inch of his skin.

Noah pushed through long vertical ropes of the slightly iridescent green kelp as he tried to keep up with the dark shadow of the retreating sea lion. He recalled the images he'd seen earlier: sparkles of light on water; the soft glow of the sun setting on the horizon.

Peace.

He glided easily in the murky depths.

In the distance a small shadow seemed to grow. What had seemed like a tiny orb only a few feet wide now lengthened to more than twenty feet. He wondered how deep he was, how far from the surface—how far away from oxygen. If he was, in fact, alive, he would need the stuff eventually.

The water became clearer as he swam closer to the darkened area. He saw a rocky exterior, tiny sea stars and barnacles affixed to jutting stone with a jagged oblong opening.

Water rushed inside the opening with the force of each wave before retreating back toward Noah. The current's force nearly pulled him back out to sea. Bubbles spun toward him before slowly push-pulling him toward the entrance near a small kelp forest that danced in exuberant splendor, pinpricks of light catching the outline of its large bulbs.

There were no sea lions in sight; for a minute Noah questioned whether he'd lost his way completely. He tried to stop, pushing the rushing water back and forth in opposite directions to keep still as he assessed whether to enter the underwater enclosure.

I could get crushed, he thought.

The booming voice made his decision for him:

"*Come.*"

Noah let go of all resistance and was pulled forward into a large underwater cave. He was filled with a sense of dread as he scissor kicked with each long stroke before disappearing inside.

32.

Jake pushed against the rigid inflatable fabric encasing the pontoons of the fifteen-foot Zodiac, moving the boat easily over a series of rollers leading to the estuary. Dry bushes surrounded the building that housed the small boats and research equipment. A trail leading to the launch area was trampled flat by the consistent march of students and faculty heading to the open waters in search of answers to the mysteries of the sea.

Tears coursed down Taylor's cheeks as she pushed the craft from the other side.

"You need to focus, Taylor, or we're never going to get out there."

"We should call my mom."

"She's incommunicado. Off-line, okay?" Jake barked. "Push the bow over to the right."

"She'd have her walkie with her," Taylor continued, grunting with the effort. "You could try that."

"She's on a dive. A deep one." Jake eyeballed the side of the craft, pointing at it with his head. "Come on, put your weight into it." Taylor pushed harder, and the vessel settled onto a set of tracks with a system of rollers that led into the adjacent estuary. "Now get back here," Jake said, "and help me get this into the water."

He loaded the craft with a long suitcase and two poles before pushing it farther into the water.

"Now climb aboard. We're wasting time."

The boat had two motors: one five horsepower engine used on the small tributary leading to the inlet and another twenty-five horsepower engine for the open ocean. Jake fired up the smaller engine and they headed out. The sun hung low on the horizon, shafts of light piercing a cluster of clouds and sparkling like diamonds on the water's surface.

"It won't be light much longer," Taylor said. "Maybe we should call somebody, just in case."

Jake ignored her and continued to steer the boat along the small waterway until they finally reached the inlet leading to the ocean.

"What if we don't find him out there? We could use some help."

Silence.

"You know, someone trained in water rescue."

"You don't understand, Taylor. He's on his own out there, but I think both you and I know he'll be okay."

"But you said Bessy's out there. That she's dangerous!"

Jake's fatherly persona cracked away, his handsome grin and devilish dimples morphing into something she hadn't seen before. Something that sent a chill skittering up her spine.

"Let's just be up front with each other here, okay?" Jake's eyes were hardened, shiny beads of disdain. "The pieces are all clicking into place. There are a few loose ends to clean up, thanks to your mom, but then the world order will shift and my plan will be executed."

"Your plan? But I thought—"

"Yes, *my plan*. And you're going to help me," he said, squeezing Taylor's right arm to accentuate the threat, "with one of the final pieces."

She smacked his hand away, rubbing the area where his fingers had dug into the flesh.

"Don't touch me."

Jake chuckled a little at that. "Don't underestimate what I can do," he warned. "What do you really know about Noah? . . . About the Trident Initiative?"

Taylor sat silently glaring at Jake. "You have no idea who you're dealing with, kid," Jake said, his gaze drilling into Taylor. "No idea at all."

Taylor looked around her, searching for an escape route, but the thought of Noah in the water kept her glued to her seat.

"Don't worry," Jake said nonchalantly, "we'll find your friend, take care of that monstrosity of a creature, and all will be well. When have I ever steered you wrong?"

***

The wind whipped up and Taylor struggled to keep her hair out of her mouth, spitting it out and pulling the thick strands back into a makeshift ponytail. Jake turned away, secure in the thought that she wouldn't jump off the Zodiac. It was his turn to underestimate the situation.

She let the vibration of the small engine carry her thoughts out over the wetlands and the activity going on around her. Small birds took flight from a clump of lavender, spooked by something unseen. A group of five brown pelicans swooped down in the distance, hovering inches above the ocean surface, their expansive wings and elongated beaks casting shadows along the water as they pursued an early evening meal. She surveyed the inventory in the small vessel: rope, poles, life preservers. Nothing she could use to overtake such a big man. She felt trapped, and desperate to help her friend. At least they both had the same goal: find Noah.

Taylor's mind was filled with questions and she was desperate to get them answered: What is Noah capable of doing? What did you do to change my mom's experiment? What do you mean, the new world order?

Taylor opened her mouth to ask, but realized everything had changed now. Any answers would not be coming from her creepy Zodiac companion.

She should have known; she'd seen the shift in his personality before, but she let her crush overcome her rational thinking. Heck, she was just a kid then, ever hopeful that he was her prince charming.

In the years Jake Stafford worked for her mom, Taylor had learned when to keep quiet when he was deep in thought, and she knew she was pushing the limits of his patience.

He had snapped at her a couple of times before.

When she was ten years old, she came to the lab for the day to hang out while her dad was at a conference. It didn't go well: Too many questions for that short period of time. It would be better not to get on his bad side, she thought. Especially when confined to tight quarters.

She rubbed her arm again, anger bubbling below the surface of her skin as she contemplated what to do. She shifted in her seat, focusing on the waves in the distance, looking for her friend, her mind racing.

I'm not going anywhere but out there with this jerk, she thought, because if I'm on a boat, Noah, I will find you.

***

The quiet patter of water from the beginning storm was stifled as Noah exploded from the water. Gasping for air and groping for a foothold on the slab of rock jutting from the side of a sandstone dome, Noah pulled himself halfway out of the water. The inside of the cave was expansive. A massive arched ceiling was open at the top with a three-foot gash, exposing the storm clouds converging above, blocking large swaths of a pink and orange sky. Raindrops were lit by the last gasp of daylight as they softly poured into the enclosure. The shimmer of the dim glow from above illuminated the cave's wet craggy surface.

The dark enclosure was suddenly filled with the deep echoes of barking sea lions and the gurgle-growl of seals, the air thick with the musty smell of their coats. The soft buzzing sound returned inside his head as he pulled himself further out of the water. The delicate flesh between Noah's fingers caught on tiny shells embedded in the gravelly surface as he groped for better footing. The dark shapes hidden in the shadows began to take form as his eyes adjusted to the darkness. At least seven harbor seals formed a loose semi-circle around him, the largest tucked against a large stone overhang at the back of the ledge.

The seal let out a low undulating growl, its head tilted toward the sliver of the last moments of sunlight streaming in from above. Noah shoved his hands against his ears, trying to stop the pounding thrum of the seal's guttural cry. It felt like his skull would crack from the pressure. He welcomed the familiar buzzing sound, grateful for the ambient noise that cut away the sharp tone of the seal.

Noah looked around at the others. "Well? What do you want?" His loud voice echoed inside the chamber. "Why am I here?"

One of the smaller seals, light gray in the dimly lit cave began to move, its entire body acting as one giant muscle, undulating its girth toward Noah who tried to scramble to a safer spot on the ledge. As it approached, the seal seemed to smile. It got within a few inches of Noah's face and let out a chuffing puff of air. Then it barked, making Noah jump. He pushed himself farther onto the ledge to avoid falling into the water.

The small seal nudged Noah's shoulder with its head, pushing him toward the larger seal at the back. Noah looked at the darkened form, which was at least six feet long, but he didn't move toward it. Although he'd seen seals and sea lions swimming beneath the dock at the marina many times before, he was unsure how they would react this close to a human, and he stood petrified, his confidence melted into a puddle around him.

The smaller seal grunted and pushed lightly against Noah's shoulder once more. The other seals began to move away from him, as if cutting a path for him to follow on the slippery ground.

Not wanting to fall off the ledge, Noah slowly began to crawl toward the larger creature, his body now shaking uncontrollably from the cold. As he came closer, he began to see more detail on the creature's spotted pelt. Its large head was regal, long whiskers fanned out from its nose and deep wrinkles of flesh draped the back of its neck. Near one flipper, a deep gash glistened, fresh blood coagulating inside the wound. As Noah approached, the large seal rumbled, but stayed completely still.

Within the creature's eyes, Noah sensed a great wisdom and immediately felt as if he should avert his gaze. The smaller seal gave him another nudge and inched closer. Without thinking, Noah reached out with a webbed hand, wanting to comfort the large seal.

"Easy . . . easy," he said, not quite sure if he was talking to the seal or to himself. As he brought his hand closer, he felt a connection to this creature. His mind was filled with a stream of images, as if the creature was offering its life's story for Noah to review before it passed. It made him think of the Spock character in the Star Trek series and the mind meld.

"Oh, my God," Noah whispered as he watched the gaping wound ooze. As Noah pressed his hand against the flesh, the seal's regal head fell to the floor. Hidden behind the seal was Kate Borcelli, knees tucked tightly to her chest, shaking with cold, unconscious but breathing.

"What the hell is going on," he whispered to himself.

As if in response, the chamber erupted with the barking cries from the group of seals around him.

33.

Detective Gomez pushed the fast forward button on the video recorder one more time. He watched as Kate Borcelli climbed on board Jake Stafford's boat. Watched them load large tubs of something. And watched the boat head out of the marina. When the boat came back, no sign of Dr. Borcelli. Just Jake.

"So, are you going to arrest him?" Zeke asked from behind the detective. He was having trouble hiding his enthusiasm about the prospect.

"This isn't proof of a crime, Zeke. She could be on the boat right now. Or they could have dropped her off somewhere. You've been after this guy for so long, I think you'd cry murder if he threw a crumpled Snickers wrapper on the ground." But the detective hit rewind once more.

There was something strange about how Stafford was acting when he pulled into the slip: too many glances around the docks; too many checks of the lock to the boat's cabin door. Something needled at Detective Gomez, but he couldn't put his finger on it. He placed another call to the station.

"Did you get ahold of Dr. Borcelli yet, Sarah?"

He waited.

"How about Dr. Stafford?"

Zeke nearly danced with excitement behind him. "Jesus, Zeke! Knock it off!" the detective yelled. "Sorry, Sarah. Just dealing with an annoying witness here," he added with a warning glare at Zeke. "Let me know if you hear back. Meanwhile, I'm heading over to the marine lab."

Detective Gomez stood up and stretched, then squinted at the marina owner. "And no, Zeke. You are not coming with me."

***

Jake pulled the large suitcase onto his lap and looked over at Taylor. "You're not going to do anything stupid when we're out here. You understand? I have had a horrible day, and I don't want to add killing some kid to the list."

Taylor's eye widened, unsure of how to respond to that little gem. It was amazing that she still felt hurt when he called her a kid, still felt an ounce of attraction for this guy. Would he really consider killing her? He's got to be joking, right?

She simply nodded, desperately looking for anyone on the water who might notice a young girl alone with an older man in a research vessel and call the cops. The ocean seemed expansive, quiet and deserted.

The only person out here that could save her was herself. She was on her own.

The Zodiac bounced along the surface of the waves, shooting fine spray from the sides as it pushed farther out to sea. Jake pulled out his phone and clicked on the GPS app. A green light illuminated on the screen, pulsing on a map. "We're close," he said.

The Zodiac continued its journey out to sea before jutting back a few miles north. From this distance, the stately rock formations seemed like children's toys cast aside in the water after a day at the beach. Taylor sat shivering in her seat as spray from the sides of the boat dashed into her face in a fine mist. "There's no way Noah got out this far," she said, her teeth chattering.

"Trust me," Jake said, squinting at her sideways.

"I think we both know that's proving to be a pretty bad idea."

Jake shifted the throttle to neutral and began pulling items out from under the side benches: several coils of rope, a spear, and a large case that looked like it could fit a saxophone. The hinges on the suitcase made a harsh squeak when he opened it.

"What's that?" she asked.

"We're stopped now, and you're going to help me find the asset that your mother lost."

"You mean Bessy?"

He ignored her question, tightening the rope around the end of a three-pronged anchor and dropping it over the side. The sun was setting and its reflection was captured on the small ocean waves as they bumped against the hull.

"I thought we were out here to find Noah?" The seawater's salt air and grit stung her skin and she gently dabbed her mouth with the back of her sleeve.

"We have a more pressing situation, kiddo."

"Quit calling me that!" she screamed.

"Sorry," Jake said with a lecherous grin. "Maybe I can find some tape in my tackle for that big mouth of yours."

Taylor sat in stunned silence, a tear making its way down her cheek. She wondered how she could have been so wrong about this guy. She looked out at the undulating sea around her. Where are you, Noah? She wanted to scream his name, but she didn't have the nerve. She felt helpless.

Jake turned the case, revealing what looked like a rifle, with three small harpoons tucked into velvet grooves, each tip ending in three curved, serrated barbs. He carefully placed it in the open case so it wouldn't puncture the Zodiac's pontoon.

Taylor's heart raced as she watched him rotate the weapon, checking each barb for sharpness. "What's that for?" she asked, her voice quavering.

"You're always full of questions, aren't you, ki—Oh, sorry . . . your majesty." He chuckled as he clicked one of the harpoon spears into the end of the rifle barrel. "Hey, I'm not going to shoot you with this . . . unless you piss me off." He winked again and began to chuckle, like it was the funniest thing he'd ever heard.

Taylor glared at him. "You're crazy."

Jake came up so close that Taylor could smell the signature hint of a mint on his breath. "No, princess. I'm a genius. And don't you forget it." He flicked her nose with his finger before sitting back in the swivel chair near the Zodiac's control panel. He slipped the harpoon under one arm and pulled out his phone, checking the GPS for an update.

They were far enough out in the water that Taylor knew her cries for help would go unanswered. She couldn't see anything to use as a weapon—nothing to overpower this man, who was easily twice her size. Taylor surveyed the boat more closely. The bench seats at the stern offered no way to hide, the middle console where the captain steered the boat didn't offer any clues to how she was going to get out of this mess. It was an open hull with a deep V floor at the bow, simple and utilitarian. And small.

Her thoughts were dire: No way out.

34.

A jumble of images flooded Noah's mind as he sat on the damp cave floor, stroking Taylor's mom's hair: flashes of blood and bone, fangs lashing in a frenzy.

"What happened to you?" he whispered.

He could feel Dr. Borcelli's body tremble as she struggled to take each breath. Noah knew what he was doing was soothing her, but he also knew he needed to get her help, and fast.

But how?

Once again he was struck by how focused the other seals seemed to be on him, and he felt a kinship with this newfound family.

Kate's body had a series of gashes along her side, but they didn't seem too deep. They were bloody, but not seeping blood. It didn't seem like any arteries had been hit, thank God.

Noah surveyed the cave, the glistening sides smooth and rounded from years of exposure to pounding surf. Tiny skeletons held firm in long cracks on the wall that had formed after massive tectonic plates pushed hard against each other deep in the earth. Noah thought he saw something stuffed into one of the crags of the wall behind Kate. He softly rested her head on her arm, and inched closer, unsure of his footing. He crawled with webbed fingers splayed along the slick surface, the musty odor of the algae-covered stones filling his nostrils.

Grabbing rubber straps, Noah tugged hard to drag it back to Taylor's mom. The pack was heavy, its side zippers hidden inside a rubber gasket to keep it watertight. All trepidation gone, Noah searched the seams to find a way to open the pack, now curious who would stick this down here in the first place. Velcro sides secured the flap that covered the zippered compartment. As Noah ripped the edges apart, the sound reverberated through the dank underwater cave.

Noah slowly pulled the contents free from within a rubber bladder sewn inside the pack. The bulk of the backpack was filled with stuff needed for survival: fresh water, canned food, an opener, a snorkel and mask . . . and a first aid kit.

The group of seals quietly stared at him.

One of the smaller seals let out a loud bark that echoed off of the cavern walls. Images flashed: a woman helping a child up from the sand; a man pulling a child on a surfboard. The voice filled Noah's head.

"*Help us.*"

"Help you do what?" Noah asked.

The seal barked again. The images were more gruesome this time. Noah still wasn't sure if he was hearing a voice, or if he intuitively knew what the seals were trying to say:
"Help us kill the beast."

***

Taylor's mom had always warned her about going into private rooms alone with strange men, but she never mentioned avoiding boat rides with creepy geneticists who played with spears.

A depth finder near Jake was turned on, its green light shining from the square black box. Next to it was a CB radio.

Help.

Taylor looked up at the darkening sky, the storm clouds receding in the distance, the strong wind blowing her dark hair east, then west, changing directions quickly.

"Storm's turning," Jake said, as if reading her mind. He walked to the bow of the boat to pull out some rigging and Taylor wondered how she could overtake him. She watched him as he connected a hoist to the side of the boat near Taylor, and wondered why that would be necessary. What are we doing out here?

After securing the rigging, Jake pulled up the anchor and returned to his seat, putting the engines into gear, slowly heading west, away from shore. "Stay calm and this will all work out fine. But if you cause any trouble, I can just pitch you over the side, and you'll be fish bait—just like your . . ."

Taylor's eyes were slits of distrust. "Like my what?"

"Just stay put and don't cause any trouble."

"What about Noah?" Another tear of frustration tracked down Taylor's cheek. She pointed at the radio.

"Can you at least check in with your security guards? Maybe they found him, and we don't need to be out here."

"For someone who comes off so smart, you're not impressing me right now." Jake pushed the throttle down farther, causing the boat's bow to rise above the surf. He yelled over the engine noise. "We're out here on a larger fishing expedition, ki—Taylor. Your friend is a secondary distraction. He'll be fine.

"We spent long hours identifying certain DNA strands, looking for specific triggers that change the course of fetal development. It's the trigger that's the key, you know. The trigger for mutation that caused such an uproar when people thought parents would engineer the perfect child who would get straight A's in all their classes, excel at sports and take over the world. But that type of engineering just gets you the same group of morons out there trying to make a buck, and killing the world in the process. The really important mutations we were uncovering—now that's for the future of humanity."

"You're both nuts."

"Are we, Taylor?" Jake's eyes twinkled in the early evening light. Taylor could swear she could see a spark of insanity shining brightly in his cornea before winking out. "Think about the situation we're in these days: pollution in the waters, mercury in chips that drive everything from our washing machines to our vehicles. And where do these chips go when people throw them out?

"And don't say they're recycled!" he screamed.

Taylor flinched as if Jake had struck her. He continued his rant. "Even in this country, with all the recycling programs in place, all the precautions and federal restrictions, people are lazy and greedy. Mistakes are made. It's only a matter of time before we kill off the oceans. Think, Taylor . . . think," he said, punctuating his point by jamming his well-manicured index finger into his forehead. "The oil spill in the Gulf of Mexico caused the near extinction of hundreds of species, and the decimation of wetlands; the Environmental Protection Agency tested fish in two hundred and ninety one streams and waterways in the U.S. for mercury, and every fish tested showed signs of contamination. Coral reefs are disappearing; people are using the oceans as dumping grounds. We were on a train ride to the end, kid. Your mom helped start the process toward our salvation. I just added the necessary touch—I had the guts to push it to the next level. It just might save the world."

"You need to take a pill, or something?"

"Now we just need to do a little cleanup," he said, ignoring her. "And you and your little boyfriend out there are going to help me do it."

"We don't even know if Noah's okay!" Taylor exclaimed. "How do you expect him to help you, if we can't find—"

"I know you saw the report, Taylor. The night of the party . . . you left the printer on."

"I don't know—"

"I know you downloaded the file. You saw Noah's name on the report. He's out there, but he won't need help. He was made for the ocean. But there are still things you don't know."

Jake waited an anticipatory grin, eyes wide, like he was a teenage girl with a thrilling secret he was dying to share.

"So?" Taylor prodded, crossing her arms, not taking the bait.

Jake tightened his gaze. "Your enthusiasm is underwhelming." He sat silently, looping a tree trunk of a leg over the back of the captain seat, gauging whether to go on or not. His ego overcame his desire to make her wait.

"You know my background."

Taylor tried her best to look bored.

"The DNA sequence I edited, and how I manipulated the strand, connected them genetically . . ."

"Yeah? So what?"

"So if Noah comes to us," Jake snapped, "I'm betting that she will come after him."

Taylor's brow knitted in worry. She'd seen the creature at the lab before. It was severely deformed, but much larger than the sea lion in the tank she took Noah to see on his birthday. "Why do you need the harpoon? Why not just have my mom call her?"

"We tried that recently, but it didn't work."

"Is that why she's still out here?"

Jake looked out over the choppy water, scanning the empty horizon. "In a way." As he began to push the throttle forward, the Zodiac lurched, the engine whining before cutting short.

Jake quickly shut off the engine, and looked over the side.

"Damn."

A portion of a crushed metal hull attached to a wooden seat struck the side of his boat with each lapping wave. "What the hell?" A rope extended from underneath the wreckage. "Dammit," he repeated, grunting as he pulled at the rope. "Sucker's caught on the propeller. Help me out, will you? I don't want this debris to puncture the hull."

Taylor looked out at the slate gray sky, veiled streaks of dark clouds dipped near the horizon as the storm retreated, the white caps on the ocean jumping and jiving around them. She had never felt so alone.

Even the seabirds had retreated and Taylor felt enveloped in the deathly silence. Where are you, Noah? She helped Dr. Stafford work to free the rope from the propeller.

"Does my mom know I hacked into her computer?"

"Don't worry," he said. "She doesn't know a thing."

35.

Noah pulled the first aid kit from the backpack and found a large roll of gauze, rectangular pads and fabric tape. He looked over at the cave entrance, the undulating sea gushed through the opening before rushing out with each swell. He sighed. There was no way he could get her out of here. He was going to need to get help.

At least I can stop the bleeding for now, he thought. He searched the lightweight plastic container and found small surgery scissors he could use to cut the gauze. He grabbed Kate's shoulder and lightly shook. "Kate? Dr. Borcelli?"

A small groan escaped as her pale lips struggled to form words. "Kate. What happened? How did you get hurt?"

Kate's eyes fluttered half open, and she tried to focus on who was crouching over her. She tried to lift herself up, but groaned louder with the pain. "Don't move," said Noah. "I need to cover your cuts. It might hurt."

Noah gently pulled her wet shirt up and away from the wounds before removing the paper packaging and placing the gauze pads over the deep gashes. He tried to dry off her skin around the bandage before he applied the tape, silently hoping it would hold. Blood seeped through the gauze looking like three crimson parentheses on her side.

"Where am I?" Kate's voice was a harsh whisper, barely audible in the dripping confines of the cave.

"We're out near Natural Bridges, I think." Noah looked at the sleek brown bodies assembled around them. "The sea lions brought me here. At least I think they did."

A seal barked in agreement, shaking its head and chuffing out a blast of air.

"Help me up," she whispered. Noah grabbed her back and pulled her slowly into a sitting position. Her hair hung limply over her face, and he gently pulled the long chestnut strands away from her eyes, looping them behind her ears.

"I know this place," Kate said as she surveyed the cave. Then her eyes stopped on the large seal lying next to her, its wounds open, but no longer seeping, its body deathly still. "Oh, no." Tears spilled down her cheeks as she caressed the seal's large head. "He saved me."

"From what?" Noah asked. "The beast?"

"Who told you that?"

Noah looked at the seals gathered around them. "They did."

"I'm not following you, Noah. How did they—"

"We can talk about that later," Noah said, trying to hide his distrust, remembering the list of names Taylor had shown him.

"She's not a beast," Kate said softly. "At least she wasn't before."

"Who wasn't?"

"Bessy. One of the lab patients. A California sea lion. She was born there several years ago, but she had . . ." Kate glanced at Noah's hands ". . . abnormalities.

"I've been working with her. I thought she was going to provide a breakthrough in my research. I know I've bored Taylor to tears about my interest in communicating with marine mammals, but we had a connection. It was going really well."

"Dr. Borcelli," Noah interrupted, "was she part of the Trident Initiative?"

Kate's emerald eyes met Noah's, confusion clouding her face.

"What's the Trident Initiative?"

***

The hollow sound of Detective Mark Gomez's heavy shoes hammering on the concrete floor accentuated the emptiness of the hallway near Dr. Borcelli's office. He wondered why the front entrance had been open, why no security guards had stopped him. Something definitely was wrong.

He entered the office and noticed a tub containing several jars filled with a murky liquid. The tub looked similar to the one he saw on the video, the one Jake Stafford had been carrying from his boat. He lifted one of the jars out of the tub, holding it carefully up against the light. The substance inside began to glow when he shook it, and he wondered if this stuff was safe to hold.

He put it back inside and looked around the area. The computer was off, but a notebook sat next to the monitor, small detailed script filled the pages. The detective quietly flipped through the book, scanning each page. He came to a section of diagrams and graphs, of drawings and photos. There were charts with dates and locations.

He closed the book and reached for the phone.

"Hi, Sarah? It's me.

"Get detective Owens for me, will you? He needs to get down here right away."

36.

A jumble of sounds bombarded Noah's mind. Outside, the seals had erupted into a series of barks.

"Shut up, okay? What are you trying to tell me?" he screamed. He slammed his fist against the cave wall.

A deafening silence followed.

Kate shrank away from him, cowering against the body of the dead seal. "Who are you talking to, Noah?" she whispered.

"You really don't know, do you?"

She gave a puzzled look in reply.

Noah sat down, his legs crossed, sighing heavily before continuing. "I don't know where to start." He looked at the semi-circle of animals around him and blew out a puff of air. "The Trident Initiative seems to be something involving a new gene editing technology. Somehow, I think, someone messed with my genes. Before I was born. Does that make sense?"

Kate continued to stare blankly.

"I think Taylor called it crispy, or something."

Noah could tell the word struck a chord.

"CRISPR," Kate said.

"Yeah, that's it! Taylor said it could be used to change a person's DNA strand. Edit out stuff, put new stuff in."

"What stuff, Noah?"

Noah looked around at his captive audience of seals and sea lions. "Their stuff, I guess. I can hear them, Dr. Borcelli. I understand—at least some of what they're saying. And swimming—"

A tear spilled down Noah's cheek, the frustration of everything that had happened building to a breaking point.

"I thought it was you," he said.

"What do you mean?"

"We found information—about the project that was going on at the lab. It was all there. On your computer, in your files. We both saw it."

"Oh, God. Noah, I had no idea. Before I hired Jake, he worked at the St. Francis Fertility Clinic."

"Where Taylor was—"

"Yes, that's where her father and I went. We were struggling to have a baby, and your mom—well, she said they were a well-known fertility clinic, known for a high success rate."

"So why isn't Taylor different too?" Noah held his hands in front of his tear-streaked face. "Why just me?"

"What's been happening, Noah? Tell me everything."

Noah explained about the voices, about the fish jumping from the tanks, the dolphins. He could tell that Kate was struggling to concentrate through the pain, was pushing herself to absorb everything Noah was saying.

The buzzing sound returned to his head, a persistent hum that drilled into his temples. The small group of seals began their undulating move, inching closer.

"I keep hearing them," Noah said, looking around him. "They're asking for help. But I don't know from what." Noah's eyes softened as he surveyed the animals surrounding him. Each had small gashes of some kind; each looked like they'd been hurt physically, emotionally. It was like they had all been in battle. But what were they fighting?

"What happened to you out there Dr. Borcelli? How did you get these gashes?"

"It was Bessy, but I swear she wasn't trying to attack me. She would never do that."

"Then how did you get these?" Noah pointed to the bloody gauze.

He could tell Kate was trying to think of an answer when a seal suddenly broke through the lapping water next to the cave entrance. It vaulted itself onto the ledge and dropped something at Noah's feet.

What now?

It looked like a tangle of brown seaweed, but as Noah pulled the vegetation aside, he saw the spear, weathered and rusted at its three-pronged tip. The seal picked up the broken handle in its mouth and began to tap the spear against a rock—*tap, tap, tap, tap*—then it dropped the spear and dragged it across the ground. It bumped along the uneven surface in one long scrape.

"That's the same type of harpoon Dr. Stafford was going to use on Bessy. We were out looking for her, when he—"

"He what?"

"We were fighting. I fell overboard." Kate winced as she reached for the spear, twirling it slowly for a close inspection. "He was going to shoot her."

Kate placed the spear gingerly onto the floor of the cave ledge. She told him about Bessy, the body found on the beach, and their boat ride to find her.

"Dr. Stafford didn't try to save you? Didn't jump in after you?"

"I don't know . . . maybe." Kate looked ashen, the soft reflection of the water casting a sickly green hue on her face. "All I know is I set her free and she killed someone; it's all my fault. I remember falling in, but nothing else. She's still out there, Noah."

Noah looked more closely at Kate's wounds. "How would she do that?"

"She has six-inch claws, Noah. And they're razor sharp."

Kate leaned back against the cave wall, exhausted. "We have to find her," her gaze pierced into Noah with its urgency. "You have to stop her. Before she kills again."

The newest seal inched closer until it could nose the spear; it began to slowly roll it with its nose until it was at Noah's feet.

The deep voice once again boomed inside Noah's head: *"Help us."*

***

Jake strained as he tugged at the rope stuck on the propeller. He grabbed one of the spears, thinking he could attach a knife to the end and saw the rope free. "Help me out here, Taylor. Find some duct tape or something in that tub over there." He leaned over, straining to reach the underside of the rope but it didn't budge.

Then he saw the shadow moving quickly toward him.

Jake scrambled backward, but his arm got wedged between the engine and the heavy rubber hull. He tried to grasp what he was seeing, but all that seemed to register was a gaping maw of jagged teeth.

He had been in dangerous situations before. One time he had come within inches of getting his middle finger bitten off by a moray eel, the digit hanging by the back half of the skin, everything else severed.

But even then he had remained calm.

He had even laughed about it to his friends at the bar later that day, holding up his bandaged finger in mock "screw you" fashion. Jake laughed about it, and said, "You see how that thing almost clipped my only ability to tell someone to go screw themself in sign language?"

This time, however, was different. No joke. Just jagged and gnarled teeth coming at him from below the debris as he frantically tried to free himself from the rope.

He felt the cool, slimy pelt as it rocketed past his arm, jaws snapping for a connection. Taylor saw it come out of the water, something unreal, and realized the water was no longer a means of escape: she was trapped on the boat.

And Noah was still out there in the water . . . with it.

37.

The sound was deafening as Noah lifted the spear from the ground. The seals and sea lions that surrounded him barked in unison, almost as if singing out a battle cry. Noah looked at his new companions in confusion.

"Help you how? I don't even know how to throw a baseball straight, let alone kill something with a spear.

"Where did you even get this?" he asked the seal that had just arrived. It blinked and blew out a puff of air in response before nodding its head toward the water.

Water dripped from the ceiling, the wet cadence marking the silence. "Why won't any of you say anything?" Noah screamed in frustration, his voice echoing through the caverns to his left.

The smaller seal that had dropped the spear at his feet shuffled itself to the edge of the rocky formation and dove into the water. It bobbed at the surface and barked one echoing call. Noah was learning to distinguish different sounds and octaves. He knew what the seal was saying.

"Come."

The thought of diving back into the frigid water made Noah start to shiver, but he stepped closer to the edge, peering over the side to look at the rushing tide pushing in and out of the cave.

Kate grabbed his ankle with her slender fingers. "If you can communicate with her, don't hurt her."

"I'll try, okay?" Noah blew out a puff of air and tucking everything he found inside the backpack before pulling it on and clasping the security strap around his waist. The seal barked at him again, obviously growing impatient.

"I'm coming, I'm coming," Noah muttered. Another seal barked, its deep tone echoing off the walls, its head nodding in agitation toward the weapon. Soon others began to move along the wet ground, their muscular chests rolling and shifting to gather momentum until they were crushed together in an encouraging wall of flesh, staring at Noah with what looked like a mixture of fear and wonder.

The small seal slapped a flipper into the water, splashing Noah in the face and barked at him one more time.

I don't need to understand seal to know what that means, he thought.

He yelled with newfound confidence, "I told you I'm coming!"

A voice responded, nearly splitting open his skull with its force: *"COME!"*

He turned to Kate, taking one last look around. "I'll bring help," he said.

Then he took several deep breaths, gripped the spear tightly, and jumped in.

***

The water bit into Noah's skin as he swam. His eyes tried to adjust to the gloom of the underwater moonlight filtering in near the mouth of the cavern. He had taken a deep breath before plunging into the water, but he noticed his chest didn't have the tightness like before. A tingling sensation coursed through his body, and although his extremities felt the cold, his chest felt warm and loose as if he'd just awoken from a long nap.

Something was changing.

He could see the forest of kelp dancing in the distance and wondered how he had gone from simply reading at his desk this morning, to holding a harpoon spear and going on the hunt for something that would probably kill him.

The dark forms of three seals left the safety of the cavern and ventured into the waving plant life, spinning their bodies around the long ropes of dancing vegetation, tiny bubbles twirling in their wake.

Well, here goes, Noah thought as he kicked off toward the departing creatures.

The harpoon would make swimming difficult for anyone, but his misshapen fingers made it even more difficult to grasp the slick surface, not to mention the added burden of undulating seawater and vegetation.

Shifting his position to being more upright, Noah pushed the end of the shaft through the loop created by the backpack strap until the sharp end stuck out just inches from his belly. He scissor kicked his legs and pushed through the water with cupped hands. He realized that it might be difficult to pull out the spear if he needed it quickly, but it wouldn't do him any good if he dropped it to the sea floor or got it tangled in the ropes of vegetation along the way.

The three seals had stopped in the distance and looked back at him steadily as they floated several feet below the surface. Noah felt a mild sense of irritation at their apparent impatience.

I'm coming, already, he mentally replied. *Lighten up. I'm only human. At least,* mostly *human.*

The smaller seal let out a bubbly bark before turning to lead the rest forward again.

The moonlight pierced the water in deep shimmering shafts of white, lighting up areas of the ocean in hues of green and deep blue as Noah swam forward.

A small school of shiny silver herring glistened as they flitted past him. He kicked through the kelp, his arms tight to his sides as he mimicked the harbor seals' movement. His ears were filled with a gurgling, popping sound punctuated with tiny squeaks, like a distant echo of a leaky rusted faucet as it dripped and groaned from the water pressure.

As he moved swiftly forward, a dark shadow darted in his peripheral vision. He stopped and turned, fighting the urge to inhale the salty water.

Floating within the waving ropes of seaweed, Noah waited, his senses heightened. Although completely wet, the hair on his arms stood at attention, his eyes widened to let in as much light as possible. Seeing nothing, he turned back and began to swim again, searching the iridescent water for the seals in the distance.

He wondered what this beast could be. What was he heading into? A mental montage showing the larger seal's wound from different angles flashed in quick succession and he thought his mind must be playing tricks on him. Fear coursed through his veins, but he willed it away. He kept reminding himself, they believe in me.

Another dark shape passed overhead.

Noah felt completely exposed.

You guys could have filled me in a little better, he thought as he looked around for some type of camouflage or shelter. *This royally sucks.*

From the distance, he could make out a large form and it seemed to be moving slowly toward him. The shadowy figure seemed to materialize in the distance as it closed the gap.

Hearing only the pounding of his heart, and an occasional ticking squeak, Noah slowly pulled out the harpoon from his belt loop. Pushing away thoughts of uncertainty and fear, Noah treaded silently in the dancing moonlit water and mentally prepared himself for battle.

***

The large shadowy figure seemed to materialize in front of Noah as it glided through the dark murky ocean. Noah was mesmerized as the creature came closer; he could make out the fluke at the back, and saw the large paddle-like fins flapping softly as it glided toward him.

A Humpback.

A pang of regret tugged at Noah as he thought about the gray whales at Klamath River. He looked at the large eye of the whale as it swam next to him, wondering if it knew—if all species of whales could communicate. If they knew more than humans would ever know.

Noah mentally pushed out a thought: "I'm sorry," thinking of images that depicted his sense of failure from that day at the river. The Humpback calmly swam on and Noah followed closely. It seemed kind and gentle as it glided through the water. Noah was sure of one thing: It understands. Without any words exchanged, Noah knew he was forgiven.

The giant creature's song reverberated through Noah, its low humming melody reminding him of when a bow is pulled slowly over a cello's strings. A voice, much deeper in tone than the other he had heard with the seals, boomed inside his head.

"Follow."

As the dark form slowly swam ahead of Noah, its eye shifted up and down, seemingly checking over the teen's body as it began a large looping turn. Noah pointed up to the surface, and directed one word toward the creature with every ounce of his newfound ability.

"Air."

He began to kick toward the surface. The whale slowly flipped its tale and dove beneath him.

I'm not following you, big guy, Noah thought. I need to breathe.

He held the spear tight to his side and kicked harder, his mind urging him up to the open air above. His quickly moving legs slammed into something that felt like hard clay, slightly giving in nature, but firm. As Noah's mind tried to process what his legs had hit, he could feel himself being pushed upward by whatever it was. He tried to keep his balance, and put one arm straight up to help cut through the water.

His hand punctured through the ocean surface, the chill night air stinging his skin. His lungs burned as he took a deep gulp of air. Noah hadn't realized how warm he felt underwater until he was out of it. He scissor kicked and moved one arm back and forth as he took a look around.

He could see a boat in the distance.

Taking a deep breath, he prepared to call out, but the whale's fluke slapped the top of the water and the large creature rolled on the surface toward him. Noah dove down to avoid getting crushed and heard the whale song once again filling his mind with the booming request once more.

The large whale dove below the surface and the whale song became stronger.

Noah looked around him; he and the whale were no longer alone. Four others had joined them, their gray mouths covered with barnacles, their fins combing the water to keep them in the same spot, hovering just a few feet from Noah.

In his mind, he screamed out at the creatures surrounding him. *What do you want?* He slowly flipped himself around. *What do you want me to do?*

A shrill screech slammed through Noah's brain. His mind reeled as he tried to think what could make such a sound. The whales stayed still, looking on as if in a trance. Then the deep voice reverberated inside his head once again.

"Follow."

Slowly the whales turned and began to swim away, pushing deeper into the dark abyss of the ocean. Noah reached out and grabbed a large white flipper of the last departing whale and pulled himself over so it seemed as if he was riding on its back. His thoughts were frantic. *You have got to be kidding me. Where are we going? I'm going to need more air!*

Noah fought the urge to turn back, to swim to the boat—to safety. However, he knew he was part of something bigger now and he was having a hard time fighting the urge to find out what. He glanced at the spear he was holding and wondered what he would soon face.

The whale's dark tail fluke, the edge speckled white, pushed the water away in long sweeps, propelling Noah farther out to sea. He looked behind him from where he had come, watching the kelp forest disappear in the distance. That's when he saw two seals come up quickly, flipping and turning in the whales' wake. Above them, five dolphins leapt near the surface before darting down next to him, their muscular tails propelling them forward at an amazing speed. To Noah, if felt as if they were wild animals fleeing a forest fire. The urgency was palpable.

Noah tried to stay calm, watching the creatures swim around him in seeming synchronicity.

In the distance on the rocky ocean bottom was a small ship, its sides eaten away by years of storm surge and algae growth. Schools of tiny anchovy sped away in large groups as the whales approached.

A new voice rang through his mind.

"Hide."

38.

Jake Stafford applied pressure, trying to stop the bleeding, and continued to scan the horizon. The image of the gnashing teeth jumped into his mind again, and he began to calculate the line strength he'd need to pull it in.

This won't be easy, he thought. It's bigger now. I'll have to hit that sucker on the side and drag her for a bit.

Tucking the rope under his arm, he looked over the side of the boat to see if the debris had pushed free. He wondered how he could use that bit of wreckage as camouflage—or even as an anchor.

Worst case? I can sink her, he thought.

Taking mental measurements of the debris, he realized that if the scrap of metal hadn't had a wooden seat attached to it, he would have been bitten clean in half. Jake calmed down as he calculated. He placed the rope on the bench seat.

With the motor still disabled, and not knowing if the thing was going to come back, he began to search under the dash. "Come on, come on," he mumbled. He leaned into a storage bin and began to rummage through a mixture of tools.

While he was distracted, Taylor considered her options. Jake grabbed several serrated-edged multi-pronged harpoons, then slowly pushed one of the handmade harpoons into the gun's front cylinder, clicking it into place.

He was calm, getting into the zone. While he carefully installed the harpoon, he never lost sight of the water's edge. With the weapon fully loaded, he inched toward the side of the boat, giving Taylor a warning look.

"Stay put, and stay quiet," he whispered harshly.

Finding a good foothold before peering over the edge, Jake pulled himself up slowly, his right eye squinting through the target site as he scanned the water's surface.

Nothing.

Keeping the harpoon gun cocked and tucked under one arm, he tentatively began to pull on the entangled rope as the boat bobbed up and down between two-foot swells. His eyes never left the pitching sea as he frantically pulled on the entwined rope. It snapped free on the third pull, and Stafford pitched backward, nearly hitting his head on the engine console in the middle of the Zodiac. He cursed loudly and regained a vantage point.

"This is why we needed to destroy the rejects at the lab," Stafford said through gritted teeth. He looked back out to sea, searching for any dark shadows or movement. "I'll just wait you out," he said to the rolling waves. "Wherever you are . . .Whatever you have become."

Although now free from the debris, Jake didn't try the Zodiac's engine. He was focused on the hunt, but he couldn't see anything as he peered over the edge of the boat into the inky black water. Light rain began to fall from a single cloud overhead.

He held his harpoon gun ready, pointing randomly at the occasional glimmers of light on the water, preparing for the next assault.

39.

Noah saw it in the distance. At first he thought it was another whale, but the shape was wrong.

Is that the beast?

Occasional shafts of light cut deep into the water, wavering in ribbons, illuminating the boat's undercarriage from a few feet away. Noah was overcome with a sense of foreboding, of deep sorrow that he couldn't explain. He watched as the creature slowly circled near the hull and tried to connect with it, enter its mind, but there was no connection. Something was wrong with this thing. Noah was flooded with dark feelings, the desire to strike out at something was palpable, and he stifled the urge to rush the beast and stab it with the sharp point of the three-pronged spear now tucked back into the backpack strap.

As the creature circled far below, Noah connected with its primal urge and he watched it swim silently, just inches below the water break, scanning the empty expanse of ocean surrounding the boat. It emitted a high-pitched cry from deep inside that reverberated through Noah as he watched it push its large, misshapen fins.

Four seals floated next to Noah, almost hovering in the coldness of the ocean depths, waiting. Noah looked at the larger seal, and slowly pulled out the harpoon. He moved his head toward the creature, pointing the harpoon it its direction.

Is this it?   Is this the beast? The seals seemed to be retreating, almost as if they were being seen through a camera lens, zooming out of focus.

We have got to work on our communication skills, thought Noah.

But he wasn't afraid. He knew he was close. He knew this was where he was supposed to be. A humming in his mind filled him with a lilting feeling of comfort and all things right, like when his mom used to sing him lullabies when he had nightmares. Noah was becoming attuned to the emotions carried by the currents in this underwater world.

Long ropes of seaweed wavered in the water, distorting his vision. There were shadows, glints of light. He squinted hard, trying to get a better view of the creature, and although Noah's heart raced, his chest didn't feel tight from the lack of air. He had found a rhythm of sorts, his lungs supporting him somehow, but he knew it wouldn't last forever.

The thing seemed to be circling an area, and Noah kicked off to get closer. He pushed through a clump of dancing seaweed and saw the hull of a boat bobbing fifty feet above him on the surface. His chest began to tighten. Noah knew he would need air soon.

***

Jake thought being a scientist helped him to be a better hunter; he felt the need to get inside the mind of an animal to hunt it well, and he tried to do that whenever he got an animal in his sights and pulled the trigger.

He wanted to be the Captain Ahab of marine biology. He fantasized about becoming a guy who discovered the world's most elusive creatures of the deep, becoming rich and famous in the process. Always looking for the easy way around situations, he preferred weapons that could be fired, rather than those that required a lot of work to get the job done. It's not like he was lazy—far from it—he just thought, What's the point of working hard if you didn't have to?

He spent much of his teen years and early adulthood learning hunting techniques and shooting rifles and large caliber pistols at the shooting range. His home was littered with weapons, many secretly secured under end tables or chairs located near large windows or doorways.

He would spend hours each night mapping out strategies to combat a potential intruder in his home, or small deer that hid in the woods outside of Freetown, a small town a few miles northeast of Santiempo. While on the water, he was forever searching for the puff of white from a whale, and would often daydream about the capture. He would watch Green Peace advocates in small rubber rafts trying to stop whaling ships, and he would always root for the whalers. We were put on this earth to dominate other species, he always told himself. That's what makes us human. But now, as he slowly peered over the side of his boat, he started to change his mind a bit.

Maybe we're not all powerful, he thought. Maybe I've met my match.

He was no longer the hunter in Bambi. This time, he felt like the hunted.

In the distance, a dark shadow about forty feet long darted below the surface of the water, approaching fast.

"What do you really know about the Trident Initiative?" he asked.

"It involves CRISPR. And Noah."

Jake took a quick look over at Taylor, then back to the water's surface.

"Nothing else?" he asked.

"My mom used to talk to this woman about—how things had gone too far. I never really knew what she meant until now."

"So you know . . . about your involvement," Stafford said icily, his eyes never leaving the ocean surface.

"What are you talking about?"

"Look between your fingers," he said. "See the tiny white scars? Scars from the surgery when you were a baby? Guess you missed that part in the data, huh? If you'd only printed one more page, you would have seen your name on the list too," Stafford said, looking over with a wink. "It's been great getting to know you since your mom . . . um . . . left. I could finally see my handiwork firsthand. Your mom still has pictures of you somewhere, when you were a baby. She wouldn't give them to me. Said they were precious, but we'll find them now; and destroy them. She always felt so guilty that Noah came out first, with his, uh, imperfections. That she could fix it, outwardly. In my mind, it's Noah who is perfect, not you. You were the reject. No sign of anything unique or different." Jake's comments tore at Taylor's heart. "He's going to change the world you know," Jake continued without taking any notice of Taylor's sadness. "He'll help to create a race that can live in a water environment."

"Wait. You tried CRISPR on me?" Taylor asked, studying the skin between her fingers.

Taylor dropped her voice, opening and closing her hands as she softly spoke, as if in a trance. "It makes sense now. I used to hide a lot around the lab when I was bored," she continued, almost to herself. "One time I heard you fighting with this weird looking lady. You were yelling about changes that might happen. I thought you were talking about the seals, but you weren't, were you?" She didn't wait for a reply. "When you were talking about ruining our ecology and destroying the Earth, you weren't concerned about marine mammals—you were planning something bigger."

"Very good, Taylor. A-plus."

"The woman talked about changing things so we could thrive in a mercury-laden environment. I thought you were just ranting about climate change again. Something my mom always seemed to end up talking about. The woman talked about controlling fetuses, but you weren't just talking about seals, were you?"

Stafford looked at her from across the boat. "Thanks to me, the hypothesis evolved—a term that's kind of ironic given the circumstances."

"What do you mean?"

"Like I told you before, Dr. Fields is a geneticist—a fertility specialist. Get it?" Jake held up his hand.

"Quiet. I think it's coming."

He looked back at the water, aiming his harpoon gun at a shadow.

"She runs a fertility clinic," Jake said over his shoulder, punctuating each word, gauging if he should continue. "You know . . . with a sperm bank? For all those independent career-minded women who never found the right guy, or for couples who were having trouble conceiving, but wanted a baby. It was pretty easy once we had access to the lab. The tricky part was tracking the results."

Taylor sat stunned, a rushing sound filled her ears and pinpricks of light flashed. *Don't faint. Don't faint.*

Stafford quietly continued. "The notes your mom kept in her journal were golden. The notes about Noah . . . and you. Levels of mercury that cause fetal abnormalities, research Dr. Fields was doing on genes that trigger mutations; she's an expert on the human genome, you know. She focused on 'transgenics'—using material from other species and adding it to a host to create new organisms."

"Why are you telling me this?" Taylor asked. The weight of the information felt heavy, and it was hard to breath.

"You should know that you're possibly one of our successes," Stafford said. "Dr. Fields was known for her work in fetal development," he went on, "and the genetic triggers that can start or stop specific organ or tissue development. She seemed to focus much of her work on the eight week gestation period." Stafford looked over at Taylor, waiting for a reaction. "Did you know that until eight weeks, most fetuses still have webbed fingers and toes?"

Taylor shook her head, eyes wide as she digested what was being said. "You're lying," she said softly.

Stafford turned back to his surveillance of the water, ignoring her comment. "Well, anyway, she wasn't always met with applause by her colleagues, mainly due to the questionable ethical nature of her work.

"It all became very exciting when we decided to overlap it with what your mom was doing. Then the CRISPR gene editing technology was discovered and voila!

"If we ever find your boyfriend out there, we can confirm that the results just may be beyond my wildest expectations."

"But for now . . . we have you."

40.

The whale's song faded in the distance as Noah hid behind the wrecked ship.

I have to get air, he thought as he peeked around the slimy plank board. He looked up at the shimmering surface where moonlight pierced the darkness and wondered how he was supposed to get up there without being seen. He also realized he didn't even know what he was hiding from in the first place.

A dolphin nudged Noah's arm with its nose as it emitted some squeaks that echoed through the water. The creature moved its head as if nodding and began to swim toward the surface, then looped back to Noah and seemed to wait.

Noah grabbed the dolphin's dorsal fin and the animal took off. He gripped the hilt of the spear tighter with his other hand, worrying that it might slip free with the force of the rushing water. The dolphin leapt in a tight arc at the surface, and Noah took a quick breath. But it wasn't long enough, and his lungs screamed in his chest as the dolphin began its return toward the sunken ship.

"Wait," he thought, panic overtaking him, his grip still tight on the slippery animal. "I need more air!"

The dolphin turned almost immediately, heading back to the surface and slowed as it neared the open water. It carefully tipped Noah's body with its muscular tail, exposing Noah's head but nothing else. The storm had passed and the sky was filled with millions of pinpricks of light. The Milky Way shone brightly above him, a smear of dazzling white in the dark sky. The moon was bright and full. Noah drank in the cool night air, his entire body seeming to expand with the oxygen. Before he could take another gulp of air, the dolphin took off, dragging him below the surface at break-neck speed.

Fortunately Noah had closed his mouth before being sucked back under water and still clung tightly to the fleeing dolphin. What are you so afraid of?

Images flooded Noah's mind: gnashing teeth; swift water rushing over rocks; a school of fish shimmering as it dashed away in unison. A high-pitched chirrupy voice boomed in Noah's head, but it was going too fast. He struggled to comprehend the exact words, but the feeling was unmistakable: get out of there.

The images coming from the dolphin were different—more realistic, somehow. And the voice in Noah's head made more sense—less like a voice being spoken from behind a heavy door, the tonal quality clearer, more precise.

Noah pushed out with his mind. Can you hear me?

"Must run," the voice echoed in his mind as they neared the eerily lit planks of the sunken ship. The dolphin flipped its tail and rolled. Noah lost his grip and watched helplessly as the animal retreated.

Wait! His mind screamed out as he reached for the fleeing mammal. Don't leave me!

As he watched the light grey animal disappear into the gloomy distance he heard the same high voice reverberate in his head.

"I hear you," it said.

Noah clung to the side of the ship, surveying the area around him. "But I'm not saying anything," Noah replied in his head.

"No Need. The mind . . . it speaks," the voice reverberated through his skull.

Noah wondered how he was able to stay under water so long. "How am I breathing? Why am I here?" he thought again, the excitement of actually interacting with this creature hard to fully comprehend. He thought about Taylor.

"No time. Flee," the voice echoed within.

He slowly reached down and pulled out the spear the seals gave to him, its sharp ends curved into three slivered prongs. Noah tried to imagine hurling the weapon deep into a creature that for all he knew was the size of a small ship and was covered in metallic scales. The spear seemed familiar—like something he'd seen on boats at the marina. He twirled it slowly, the streaming glints of moonlight catching the edges of the razor sharp talons on the end.

How am I going to get this going fast enough? He chuckled at that, hefting the long shaft more securely in his awkward grip, recalling all the changes in him that had materialized recently.

Noah came to the realization that the burning sensation in his chest wasn't as intense as when he first hit the waves. Things were changing, but would they change quickly enough? A foreboding song of a Humpback erupted. The ocean seemed to vibrate around him, as if shivering with its own uncertainty.

Two seals swam up from below and stayed close to his side, like some kind of Secret Service battalion. Staying hidden within the wavering stalks of vegetation, Noah began to pull himself up with one hand, the other still grasping the harpoon. Noah's eyes connected with the larger seal below, and he bobbed his head upward, pointing to where he was going. The seal released a small bubble of air and nodded its head. Noah began his ascent.

A blast of chilly wind cut into the skin on Noah's face as he broke the surface, pumping his arms back and forth smoothly while sucking in a invigorating breath of air. He could see the boat more clearly above the swells in the evening light. It rocked back and forth, riding the waves, but he could tell the engines were off. Fishermen? He could see the head and shoulders of a big man who seemed to be talking to someone sitting down. The salt water stung on his lips, and he could taste the spray coming off the small waves. The sky was brightly lit, with wisps of grey clouds streaked across it in long gashes.

Something about the man looked familiar—the tilt of his head, the broadness of his shoulders. Then he had it. It was Doc Stafford . . . and Taylor.

Noah was about to cry out to him when the large mottled grey fin of the humpback whale lifted out of the water and slammed down next to him. A seal popped up from beneath the water and gave a small sniff, nodding its head back and forth before gently grabbing Noah's arm and pulling him back under. Right before his head was completely submerged, Noah could have sworn he heard Taylor scream.

***

The water lapped gently against the slowly rocking hull as Jake inched closer to the side of the boat and glanced into the water, using the beam of the search light to cut into the inky surface. Something hit the bottom of the boat with three small thuds, like the hull was being smacked with a tennis racquet.

Jake leaned over the side, trying to get a better look at what might be underneath them. The beam of light cut through the dark water undulating in slow ripples against the sturdy ribbed hull. The white light lit up two large forms gliding smoothly just inches below the surface. A third form followed closely after.

"Seals," Jake said as he let out a sharp laugh while he turned to look at Taylor. "It's just a bunch of—"

A shrieking cry pierced the night as a dark figure leapt from the water five feet away from the boat. Steely teeth reflected the moonlight as the thing twisted before falling back to the surface. Stafford swung his searchlight toward the sound, and caught sight of a creature that seemed to have come from the bowels of hell.

Its face was contorted with large bulbous eyes that shown green in the night. Its mouth was a gash of jagged teeth that snapped menacingly at the air. Then it was gone, the searchlight beam bobbing on the rippling water, a light red fog drifting down into the depths, the only evidence that anything unusual had happened.

Jake sat down hard on the middle seat. He looked at the distant lights and the oar, gauging the distance he would need to row to safety. He grabbed his harpoon gun tightly, like a mother with child, and leaned against the dash, his heart desperately slamming inside his chest.

"It'll be okay," he said softly in an effort to reassure himself. "It'll be okay. . . ." His eyes shifted from his cell phone to the CB radio. But he knew calling for help might alert the authorities, so he pushed the thought away.

He felt stuck, and Taylor could see that the confusion was clouding his mind. She vaulted herself at him, smashing herself against his massive chest, but only ended up bouncing off of him. Taylor fell hard onto the deck, the wind knocked out of her.

Jake didn't even flinch when she hit him; he was laser beam focused on the water . . . and he was terrified.

In a monotone, he said, "Sit back down, kid. We've got trouble and there's nowhere you can go, so just deal with it. Besides, I might need your help."

Taylor inched toward the edge of the boat and peered over. The water seemed calm, welcoming.

The chilly air bit hard into Taylor's exposed skin and she shook violently, her teeth chattering a quick cadence. A strong cool breeze blasted her face and tears of frustration streamed down her cheeks.

"Oh, man . . . I'm . . . in tr-tr-trouble," Taylor chattered to herself as she peered farther over the edge. She sat back down, trying to gauge her next move.

What if he's right, Taylor thought. What if I'm different?

Taylor looked closely between her fingers she could almost make out tiny lines where the incisions had been made. She flexed her right hand much like she'd seen Noah do so often over the years. She could almost hear her friend's laughter, and her thoughts filled with images of him. She stood up to move away from Jake, but was so focused on her hands that she never saw what hit her.

The creature slammed hard into the side of the boat, pitching it sharply to the right—and tossing Taylor over the side.

41.

The biting chill sliced into Taylor's bones as she hit the water and dropped below the surface. Her thoughts splintered off in different directions as she tried to comprehend what had just happened. She couldn't tell which way was up, and she felt her chest tightening with fear.

A dark shadow crossed a few feet overhead, but it was gone before she could clearly make out its shape. From the distance, she could make out squeaks and intonations so many marine animals used to communicate. It was like they were all going crazy. Her mind tried to grasp what was happening.

Taylor's body became entangled in the long strands of kelp that brushed against her skin with each ripple of the ocean's undulating current. The shift and dance of the towering stalks of vegetation was disorienting, but she tried to stay focused, her lungs burning as she swam in a trajectory away from the boat and up toward the surface. She broke through with a gasp and searched for something that she could grab hold.

Choppy waves met her wherever she looked. She scissor-kicked her legs to stay afloat. The Zodiac was still fairly close, dark in shadow against a star-studded sky. She heard the waves lapping against its hull and a bright pinprick of light danced toward her.

Taylor considered her options: Swim to shore, which was easily a few hundred feet away, or plunge under the surface, pushing upward with her hands to stay away from the boat's searchlight.

She could see the point of light turn away, but she knew it would return. And Noah was still out here.

Taylor pushed herself up enough so just her head was exposed, and took a deep breath. The boat seemed closer to Natural Bridges, now. It seemed to be drifting away.

Her teeth chattered. Numbness crept up her legs, their weight beginning to pull her back under. I can't just sit here like some kind of human buoy and sink to my death, she told herself. Get moving.

She kicked hard and struck something large. Then she felt a hard tug on her leg. She remembered the creature she had seen before she fell overboard and envisioned its teeth sinking into her ankle. She panicked, her heart hammering in her chest, and she began to kick, trying to loosen whatever had her leg, gulping down briny saltwater as she tried to escape.

Two heads punctured the surface, large eyes sparkling, staring at her merrily, long whiskers glistening in the moonlight. The thing holding her leg pulled her under and she could see the larger seal spin itself around, its face just inches from hers, its mouth agape.

It emitted a lazy air bubble that floated upward, looking like a bulbous jellyfish bobbing inches from her face. Taylor blinked twice, staring at the harbor seal that was returning her gaze. The second one joined the first, lining up just inches away—a smaller mirror image. Taylor stared back, wondering if this was how they would stay forever. She kicked toward the surface, bursting into the chilly air and gasping for a breath. But she didn't feel threatened. Although the animals were large, they seemed genuinely happy, almost playful. The larger one let out a loud bark in a quick hello.

The shrill cry she'd heard before echoed through the night and the seals turned in unison toward the sound. The smaller seal used its head to nudge Taylor's body away while the larger one circled beneath her, gently grabbing her ankle with its mouth and pulling her down.

Taylor fought panic.

She knew right away what they were trying to tell her.

Without hesitation, she took a deep breath then wrapped her arms around the smaller seal, letting it carry her into the ocean depths.

***

Jake looked over the side, grabbing his harpoon gun and securing a search light attachment to the scope. He switched off the alarm, the silence enveloping him.

The moon was reflected brightly on the waves, a rippled line of light shimmering toward the horizon. The multipronged arrow and shaft secured in the harpoon gun connected to a long rope tied off on the boat's stern.

He scanned the water's surface, but the moonlight played tricks with his mind. The white reflection on the waves and shadows created in each swell made it difficult to be sure what he was seeing. He should have switched his scope to night vision, but he should have done a lot of things differently. Jake readjusted the harpoon gun, not caring about the fact that a misguided shot could kill Taylor.

"Come on you stupid mutant," he whispered, squinting into the wavering ocean surface. "Come on, come on. I'm right here. This way. . . ."

He heard an unearthly scream in response.

His cell phone on the console began to buzz. He knew who was calling, what they wanted him to do. But he wasn't listening anymore. He knew a text would follow shortly: abort.

A large shadow appeared three feet below the water surface. "Abort this," Jake said as he squeezed off a shot.

42.

Noah couldn't believe what he was seeing when Taylor appeared through the long strands of kelp, holding tightly onto the chest of one of the small harbor seals that he'd seen near the cave entrance. Taylor didn't have scuba gear or a snorkel, and she looked panicked. The seal sped off toward the cave entrance and Noah quickly swam after it.

Noah couldn't seem to move his arms fast enough.

Hold on, Tay, I'm coming, he thought as he pushed forward with one hand, the other still clasping the shaft of the harpoon.

She doesn't hear me, Noah said to himself. He wasn't surprised, but still he was hoping his newfound form of communication would be universal, available to everyone. Once he unlocked the secret to the clicks, whines, burps and moans, it all made perfect sense, like the first time you sound out a word phonetically, and then you could read.

Foot-long strands of slimy seaweed passed in front of him as he propelled himself through the dense green forest, and he kept the harpoon tight to his chest as he swam, ensuring it wouldn't get tangled in the long strands. One image played over and over in his mind: Taylor holding on tightly with one arm, her eyes closed, mouth slightly open as the seal pushed its flippers through the briny depths.

Don't be dead, he thought. Just hold on.

He kicked himself forward through the salty water, spinning himself as he had seen the seals do. It seemed to propel him faster. The whales, the dolphins, even many of the seals seemed to have disappeared. His vision was focused on the small opening in the rock ahead; he was aware of nothing else.

It seemed to take forever to reach the entrance, but this time he didn't hesitate and spun himself tightly into the space, bursting up to the surface with a huge gasp, gulping the cool air, filling his burning lungs.

Taylor lay hunched over the larger stone edge. Her eyes were closed and her head rested against a slime-covered rock, but Noah could see that she was breathing. He quickly swam to her, placing the harpoon down on the rock shelf and pulling himself up before gently pulling the girl onto the flat surface of the underwater cave.

"Taylor," he said, leaning over his friend and brushing hair from her face. "You hear me, Tay? It's Noah." He waited for his friend to open her eyes, look up at him, but instead she continued with slow shallow breaths, her face looking pale in the strange underground light. Noah heard shuffling scrapes of several harbor seals as they inched closer to them.

"Stay back," Noah snapped, his stiff hand extended outward, his mind echoed the order. The seals stopped, silently bobbing their heads up and down as if agreeing to his command.

A soft groan left his friend's lips, and Noah hunched over her once again. "Tay . . . just breathe. You're okay. Just breathe."

Taylor began to cough and tried to sit up, turning to her left and nearly plunging back into the water.

Taylor's eyes slowly opened, and she propped herself up on one elbow, surveying her surroundings. She smiled weakly when she saw Noah, and she grabbed him and crushed him in a tight hug. "I thought you were dead!"

Noah grinned, trying to loosen her grip. "Nope. Alive and kicking," he said with a tight wheeze. "Struggling to breathe."

Then she heard it: her mom's voice.

"Is she okay?"

Taylor glared at her mother. "What's she doing here?"

"She's hurt," Noah said. "I think this is one of those caves out past Natural Bridges, under one of the old structures that fell down a long time ago."

"I can't believe you're under here," Kate added. "You sure you're okay? Breathing okay?"

Taylor checked herself over, looking for damage. "Yeah, I think I'm okay." She remembered what Dr. Stafford had told her, and tried to push down her anger.

Noah looked at the seals. They barked once. *Help.*

Tears of frustration and rage began to spill down Taylor's cheeks. "You were right about him, Noah. Only it's worse than you thought. He's crazy. He was saying stuff up there that— that—"

"It's okay," Noah said, wiping away a tear and a wet strand of hair that had fallen over Taylor's eyes.

A deep rumbling roar filled the expanse of the cave, silencing both of them. The cave fell deathly still as the massive sea lion from the back of the cave lumbered slowly toward them, sharp lines from its recently healing wounds glistening in the low light. Its loud bark filled the air, and the deep voice reverberated inside Noah's head.

"The beast is near."

43.

The scream echoed through the water, then was punctuated with a deep roar, causing Jake to take a pensive look over the side just as the creature struck from below.

The impact sent Jake flying, landing hard on the center console, cracking three ribs in the process. Rolling to his side, he pushed into an upright position, grabbing for the harpoon gun that had slid to the boat's stern. He extended his fingers as far as possible, each push of his legs sending a sharp pain shooting through his chest.

Jake stretched, biting his lip with the strain as his fingers brushed against the metal shaft. Darkness was engulfing the boat as clouds moved in, obscuring the rising full moon.

As the boat rolled lightly to the left, Jake was able to loop his index finger into the firing mechanism, pulling the weapon within reach. He grunted as he inched closer to the harpoon gun. "Easy . . . easy," he rasped. "Almost . . . there. . ."

The second jolt sent a stabbing pain through him as the broken portion of a fiberglass fishing rod punctured the flesh under his rib cage.

Jake scooted toward the side of the boat, grabbing a sweatshirt and tying it securely around his middle, grunting with the exertion. Then he picked up his harpoon gun and prepared for another assault.

The attack came swiftly, catapulting Jake across the deck and into hard ribbed shell of the hull. He looked up at the sky; the stars winking behind streaks of light gray clouds seemed to mock him. He thought about the creature and wondered why it wasn't continuing its attack. "She's playing with me," he mumbled, realizing he was no longer the hunter: he was the hunted.

***

"What did he say?" Taylor asked Noah.

"Who?"

Taylor eyeballed the large sea lion that waited nearby. "Him," she said. "What did it tell you? Can you understand what they're saying?"

She wondered why, after all Dr. Stafford had told her, she didn't hear what Noah was hearing. Why did she have tiny scars but no ability to communicate with them?

"Yeah, I heard it," said Noah, picking up the harpoon. "I have to go."

"What about us?"

"You need to stay here with your mom." Noah slung the backpack over his shoulders, strapping it once again around his waist. Maybe the fabric would serve as a protective vest from whatever was out there. "Once I take care of things, I'll get help."

"Are you kidding me? You're not leaving me down here; I'm going with you."

"She needs someone with her."

"Why can't we both go with you?"

Noah gave Kate a knowing look. "She's too weak and it's not safe right now."

Taylor was irritated by the interaction between her mom and Noah. "Is that all you're going to tell me? How about cluing me in on what's going on? This is not just about you and your newfound ability; or about my mom's secret project."

"Taylor—"

"No! Enough!" Taylor screamed. "Fill me in."

Noah hefted the harpoon, studying the tip and gauging the weight of the shaft. "There's no time. Your mom can fill you in."

Taylor looked at the large sea lion sitting quietly on the cave ledge and blew out her breath in exasperation.

She turned to Noah, pleading. "What did it say to you?"

Noah gave a heavy sigh, knowing the information he was about to tell her wasn't going to go over well. "They say the beast is close. I think I'm supposed to kill it or something," Noah said quietly, fiddling with the sharp tips of the harpoon.

"With that thing?" she said, pointing to the weapon.

"It's my security."

"What are you nuts? Whatever that is up there attacked the boat, knocked me over. It looked like it came from the Mesozoic Era. You can't seriously think you can kill something they call 'the beast' with a sharp stick, do you? I've seen it. It nearly capsized us."

"Well, what do you think I should do?" Noah shot back. "For all I know, these are just voices in my head and they're not talking to me at all. I'm guessing, okay? I'm going with my gut, like you told me to do with the whales." He dropped his head in defeat, before quietly adding, "And I'm not going to fail again. Whether they're really talking to me or not, I just know these guys expect me to do something to help them. It feels right."

One harbor seal barked as if in agreement.

"Would you cut that out?" Noah snapped at the seal.

"Mom! You have to tell him how dangerous it is. Tell him not to go."

Kate sat quietly absorbing this back and forth, too tired to interject, too weak to think it all through clearly. "I don't know . . ."

"She doesn't know what I can do," Noah offered. "She doesn't know about me."

"*You* don't even know what you can do!" Taylor cried.

"I'm learning, okay? There's no time to fight about this. I'm going, and you're staying here. I'll be back with help. I promise."

"How do you know? How can you promise? You're listening to voices in your head!"

Noah looked hurt. He twirled the harpoon in his hands, trying to control his emotions. Then he lifted his gaze to hers, the strength shining through his eyes. "You need to believe me; I can do this."

"What if you . . ." Taylor said.

"Okay, listen," Noah said, he unhooked the backpack and handed it to her. "There's snorkel gear over there, first aid, stuff like that." He tossed it over to her. "There's a flare gun inside. Give me some time. Let me try to take care of it. I need to take the lead, do what I think is right. But if I don't come back . . ."

Taylor hefted the backpack, looking at her friend with a newfound understanding. "How are you going get out of here? How are you going to breathe?"

"Don't worry," he said confidently. He held the harpoon like a scepter as he stood there grinning, looking much older than he had just the day before. "Doctor Adonis up there seems to have taken care of that."

Then Noah winked and jumped in the water.

44.

The water was different now: more menacing, more sinister than before. The tall stalks of wavering kelp seemed to beckon Noah with a silent siren song, calling him forward to a place he knew he probably shouldn't go—to a place of nightmares.

His heart trip hammering in his throat, Noah kicked forward looking for any signs of a beast. The fish that had been swimming lazily in the shifting waters were now gone. Only the lonely sway of the dark green vegetation showed Noah any sign of life.

He flipped in a tight swirl to check behind him before kicking forward. He was alone. His mind pushed him forward: You can do this.

The only problem was that he didn't know what he was really supposed to do.

They were telling him to stop it, so he would try.

But stop it from doing what? Why did he have to kill this thing? He thought about how Taylor described the beast, but he quickly removed those words from his mind.

Not helpful. Focus on the task at hand, he told himself.

As he pushed through the water, he wondered if he should have stayed in the cave. And he wondered if Taylor and Kate could get out safely. There was only one snorkel, one set of fins. If he couldn't get help, someone, probably Kate, would have to stay behind. And if there is a beast out here, it could get Taylor, too. He tightened his grip on the harpoon and kicked harder, resolving himself to succeed.

The harpoon's shaft felt cold against his skin and he wondered again why he didn't feel the iciness of the water. What genetic magic did they pull off that caused him to be so comfortable down here? And if he could do this, what was the beast capable of?

One thing he did know, he was running out of air. And with no beast in sight, he didn't like the idea of going to the surface to get it. His lungs began to sting slightly as he continued to hide in the kelp, his eyes searching the undulating water for any sign of movement.

In the distance, he thought he saw a dark object on the surface, but it could have just been the light playing tricks on him. Every cell in his body began to cry out for oxygen, but the dark recesses of his mind were locked down, petrified. Then survival instincts kicked in and his body took over, propelling him upward.

Luckily his attention stayed focused on the cool night air above him, and not on the dark shadow coming swiftly from below.

45.

The wind had picked up considerably, and Jake knew the rain would start in earnest soon. He needed to find Bessy before she could attack again. And while he was able to clear the rope from the propeller, he was concerned that he might come across another piece of debris like the one that had disabled it the first time.

Jake pushed the throttle down ever so slightly, listening for any signal from the sonar fish finder of something big below. The device cast a soft green glow across his chiseled features.

The makeshift bandage wrapped around his middle began to bloom with a fresh red stain where the fishing rod had punctured the skin, but Jake took no notice.

His eyes locked on the viewfinder as he drove the boat slowly in a grid pattern near Natural Bridges, wiping stinging mist from his brow to keep his vision clear. Jake knew the area well and was aware of underwater hazards that had capsized many boats in past years. He was careful to watch for buoy markers that warned of the submerged wreckage.

The storm seemed to be passing overhead, moonlight pushing out between dark heavy rainclouds.

Jake flicked on a side-mounted searchlight as he drove the boat slowly forward. In the distance he could see a twinkle of lights on the shoreline moving across the water, and he wondered if they could see his tiny pin-prick of light from there. "Better be some stupid event at the lab," Stafford mumbled. "That's all I need now."

Heavy raindrops began to fall, each fat drop making a soft and slow pattering sound on the hard ribbed surface of the Zodiac's hull. Jake wished he had taken the time to come out here on his Boston Whaler, and hoped his dog was doing okay. He knew he'd probably end up having to deal with a mess in the cabin again, but there wasn't anything he could do about that now. Things had slowly begun to spiral out of control.

He glanced at his cell phone and considered making a call to check in, but he didn't have the energy to begin to explain everything that had happened. Besides, he needed to finish the hunt.

Just as he began to think the tide was turning in his favor, the engine sputtered and died. The boat dipped inside each ocean swell as Jake surveyed the surface for any sign that he wasn't alone.

He glanced at the fish finder attached near the boat's steering wheel, waiting for the series of high-pitched beeps, a pulsing neon green light flashing from the corner of the box that would alert him of something big below. It sat dark and silent. Each crest of the rolling waves gave him a better vantage point. Not once did he think about Taylor. Not one thought went to Kate or Noah. He was focused on the hunt.

"Come on, come on," Stafford said, the boat rocking slightly in the waves.

Then the device erupted into a series of stuttering beeps before shifting to a constant shrill.

Jake slid the harpoon gun slowly over the side of the boat, using a night vision scope to search the inky black undulating water surface. Nothing. He reached up and flicked on a green LED tracer light on the harpoon's tip.

The sky cleared once again. Although the moonlight lit the water, causing it to waver and sparkle in the distance, the reflection made seeing underneath the surface difficult.

Jake's arm began to ache, the tip of the harpoon gun wavering as his muscles went into a mild spasm. The fish finder seemed to have gone haywire, emitting long beeps punctuated by a multitude of smaller high-pitched blips as if it was tracking a mass of tiny crustaceans running from something chasing them on the ocean floor.

The sound was driving him nuts, and Jake considered simply turning it off, but he knew he needed every bit of help he could get. He listened intently to the lapping waves against the hull of the boat, hoping for a sign—anything that would alert him of anything large approaching.

Then he realized the small pinprick of light that had seen bobbing on the water in the distance earlier was coming toward him. It was so close now that Jake could hear the whine of an outboard motor, growing louder as it approached. Company. That's all he needed now. He knew, at minimum, the small boat would drive away the animal. But what was a small boat doing out here? And why was it heading straight toward him?

Time was running out.

"Come on you bug-eyed freak," he whispered to the water. "Come and get me."

The fish finder responded in an elongated pulsing rhythm, signifying something big—really big—underneath the boat. He didn't have time to check. Couldn't waste seconds figuring out where Noah was on the GPS. Without hesitation, Jake aimed at what he thought must be the creature coming up from below and fired.

A loud pop shattered the stillness, followed by a tight hiss as the arrow plunged into the ocean, pulling the heavy-gauge wire attached to the harpoon with it.

"Hit, dammit. Hit!" Stafford watched the lit tip of the harpoon arrow fly in a sharp line, illuminating the water around it as it descended into the murky depths. Then it abruptly extinguished. A piercing cry, muffled by the ocean depths, rumbled from below, filling Stafford with a mixture of exaltation and dread.

Now the hard part began.

46.

Noah heard the pop and saw the light shoot toward him. Was it a rocket? If so, this was faster—much faster. He just missed being impaled by the spinning harpoon. He watched it whiz past his face, the dark line of steel rope just inches away as it sped deeper into the dark water below.

As he watched the light descend, Noah saw what was swimming toward him: gaping jaws encrusted with jagged teeth, the bulbous eyes rimmed red. The creature was just a few feet below him when the lit harpoon point disappeared into its mottled flesh. The sound of the beast's cry was deafening, but he fought the urge to cover his ears, defensively extending his own weapon tight in his right hand.

Slowly the beast began a dreadful ascent toward the surface. Someone was hauling it up, but it jerked with each pull before stopping five feet below the floating hull of a small boat. Noah saw agony in the luminescent eyes of the creature and was startled when he heard a raspy voice boom inside him.

"*Help me.*"

Noah grabbed the rope with his left hand, trying to reduce the tension, but it held firm. Using the serrated ends of his harpoon, he tried to cut through the line, but it had no effect. The creature's eyes seemed to soften as it watched Noah work.

One of the seals from the cave floated into Noah's field of vision. Noah stopped cutting at the line, waiting for some kind of instruction, but the seal just watched him with curiosity, seeming to encourage him to continue. Noah wondered why it didn't tell him to stop, to take care of this, do the final deed.

The seal let out a bubble of air, and the voice confirmed Noah's suspicion: "*Help.*"

Noah looked down at the creature below him, its jagged teeth menacingly tangled in a grimace. But when he looked more closely Noah realized the creature simply couldn't close its mouth. In fact, it seemed like this thing was having difficulty breathing at all; its entire body heaved as it tried to twist free from the harpoon and the strong line holding it.

Noah slowly pulled himself down toward the beast, using the rope to bring himself closer. Blood poured from the area where the harpoon had entered, and each tug of the line shredded more flesh. Noah wondered if there was anything he could do. He looked around him in the murky water, hoping for a sign that more help was coming.

In the distance, hiding behind wavering strands of kelp were two more creatures, their bulbous eyes smaller than the ones of the injured creature next to him, but with the same misshapen features and red hue.

Their jagged teeth were similar in size and ferocity, but there was a gentleness and desperation that Noah could feel emanating from them.

He came to a realization: "Oh God. This thing is just protecting her pups."

Pops and squeaks coming from four dolphins filled the water around him. The dark shapes of the sleek grey mammals circled around him.

"*Save us*," they reminded him. "*Save us from the beast.*"

Noah replied with his mind, "I can't kill the mother."

But the four dolphins were not focusing on the mortally wounded creature. They swam toward the boat in synchronized fashion encircling it, their snouts pointing toward the bottom of the dark hull. The voices boomed inside him once more.

"*Save us from the beast.*"

47.

Taylor heard the reverberating roar through the water as she rushed toward the surface. She griped the backpack firmly as she held onto the small seal that had brought her to the cave. The sound caused the seal to pause momentarily before it kicked off again. Taylor longed for a deep breath of air. Fiery embers began to burn in her chest.

She wondered about the sound she just heard. Was it Noah? Was he killing the creature she had seen attack the Zodiac? Or was Noah in trouble? She urged the seal forward with her mind, pushing away any thought that her friend might be hurt—or worse. *Hurry, hurry, hurry.*

Bursting into the open air, the chill of the night sliced into Taylor's lungs and she struggled to take a breath. The backpack was light, almost buoyant. It was obviously made for scuba diving and she was grateful to have it and used it as a floatation device. She looked around to get an idea of where she was and thought she saw a shadow moving toward her on the distance waves.

A boat!

She knew it wasn't the Zodiac; it was much smaller and moving fast, then it started to turn away. She scrambled for the zipper, nearly losing her grip on the backpack before snatching it up close to her chest and shifting the pack so she could access the front compartment.

She pulled out the flare gun her mom showed her before she left the cave and tried to remember the steps her mom told her: unlock the safety, point it away from you into the air.

Like most of the backpack contents, it was lightweight, and Taylor silently hoped it wasn't just some kind of prop.

She looped her arms into the backpack so it stayed under her chest, then lifted the weapon above her head and fired.

***

The sky lit up as the flare shot toward the stars, bursting in a blazing ball of flame before falling to the rocking waves below, illuminating Jake and the Zodiac. He knew he was no longer invisible. The people on board the small boat pointed in his direction as the embers from the flare descended in a fabulous arc.

Jake grunted as he turned the crank, reeling in the heavy line using a winch he had secured to the side of the boat.

He jerked the mechanism, setting the hook before continuing to pull in the creature. The bouncing light on the water shifted in his direction. He only had minutes to finish if he was going to have any chance of outrunning them.

Then he saw her: his lucky charm. Taylor was floating in the water, screaming her lungs out for help, bobbing between him and the approaching boat.

His mouth set in a deep grimace as he pushed on the crank, cursing himself for not adding a motorized component to the lift. The cable slowly began to wind itself into the boat, but the weight of his catch was too large. The side of the boat began to tilt precariously toward the lapping waves.

No longer afraid of being discovered, Jake stopped the crank and attached a light to the tip of the lever, directing it to the water below. He had to stop the crank from spinning out of control, secure it and make the final kill shot. He sling the harpoon over his should and continued to pull the creature up.

"Just a few more feet," he grunted to himself.

The fact that the cable wasn't swaying or pulling against him at all made him sure that, this time, he was going to win. He peered over the side of the boat and was surprised to see pale blue eyes staring back at him. Jake locked the crank into place and swung the harpoon off his shoulder just as ocean water smashed into his face as Noah catapulted into the boat.

48.

Noah tried to recover his footing on the Zodiac's slippery deck. A wall of water crashed over the edge of the boat when four dolphins—one of which had pushed Noah into the craft with its head—flipped high into the air and splashed down firmly onto the foamy surface next to the boat. The surrounding waters were chaotic. Seals and sea lions barked loudly, mixed with dolphin chatter.

Noah glanced around looking for his weapon, but he struggled to adjust to the darkness engulfing the boat. Jake turned the crank, ignoring Noah, intent on hauling up the creature. He muttered to himself, his face contorted with the exertion and his teeth reflected an eerie glow from the moonlight.

"If you want to help," Jake grunted, turning the crank slowly once again, "you should go help your girlfriend." Jake glanced over toward Taylor and struggled to make another revolution of the crank. The boat began to list with the weight.

"Let it go!" Noah launched himself at Jake, but it was like hitting a brick wall. "You don't know what you're doing!" Noah slammed his fist into Jake's chest, reigniting the pain in the large man's cracked ribs.

Jake shrugged Noah off with a quick movement and kicked him hard in the chest, sending him crashing against the steering column. "I know what I'm doing, kid," Jake said gruffly, grunting with another pull. "That thing's a reject and needs to be destroyed. There's no way I'm letting it go now until I know it's dead."

As Noah tried to regain his footing on the slick surface, his hand slid beneath the underside of the brown tarp secured on the ground near the stern of the boat. He felt the sides of the open plastic container, the soft wet pelt and the pinprick of whiskers tickled his fingers. Pulling away his hand quickly, as if he was bit, he unfurled the tarp, exposing the body of a mutilated seal; its mottled pelt gouged deeply, its eyes unseeing.

Noah's skittered away from the carcass, eyes wide in shock. His feet slid in a mixture of salt water, blood and slime. The harpoon was stuck in the mixture. Noah's fingers brushed the shaft, almost in reach. Then he felt a stab of pain as Jake stomped on his wrist.

Jake picked up the weapon, twirling it like a baton and pointing the three-pronged tip at Noah's outstretched hands.

"I'm sorry we couldn't figure out how to give you all the benefits of the genetic manipulation without making you look so freakish," Stafford said, shaking his head in disgust.

Noah stared at Jake with his steely blue eyes, flexing his hands open and shut, ignoring the pain in his right wrist. Then slowly, he said, "I'm . . . not . . . a freak." He kicked the legs out from under the man, and sat down hard on his chest. He picked up the harpoon that had clattered to the ground and held the sharp tips against the man's neck, adding softly, "Don't . . . move."

Noah kept his eyes riveted on Jake as he listened to the crank, now unhindered, spinning wildly, releasing the creature from the boat's grip.

From behind he heard Zeke's voice cry out. "Hold on, son! We're coming!" The sound of the approaching outboard motor buzzed loudly in his head and flashing police lights reflected off the water. Noah realized the barking of the seals had quieted.

The sound remaining in the night was the lapping of the waves against the hull, marking the seconds until his rescue.

49.

Detective Gomez sat quietly watching Jake rant in a small, dank interrogation room at the Santiempo Police Department.

"There's stuff in that ocean you don't know about," Jake said. "Something out of your control. I'm the one you need to take care of it! I can fix things; make them right. I'm the one that will keep the oceans safe, keep the human race from imploding. You have to listen to me. I'm the one. . . ." He looked off toward the corner of the starkly lit room, unable to finish his thought.

The detective shook his head, chuckling, tapping his pencil on his notepad. "Jake, we have so many charges against you, including kidnapping and attempted murder, I wouldn't concern yourself with a sea monster," he said.

"Do you understand the meaning of the word hypocrite? You want to explain the collection of mercury vials on that Zodiac? And the carcass of a protected species cut up and under a tarp? I don't think you're quite understanding the serious crap you have yourself buried in, but I must say it's fun to watch you squirm your way deeper into the pile."

The detective's partner nodded, with a grin, taking a sip of coffee from a paper cup. "By the way, Dalton picked up your dog," Gomez noted, motioning his head toward his partner. "Nice mutt."

Jake stared in stony silence.

"So, you're saving the world? Mind if you elaborate on that?"

"I'm not saying anything," Stafford fumed. "And I'm not talking to you anymore. I want an attorney."

Gomez grinned and walked out. "Suit yourself," he said, the heavy door slamming behind him.

***

Dr. Diane Fields shuffle-walked to her Mercedes and threw the stack of papers and files into the trunk, no longer concerned about order and keeping all the documentation in pristine condition. Everything was falling apart and she knew it.

The wind whipped up around the tall woman, grains of asphalt pelting her legs as she slammed the trunk and circled around to the driver's side door. She could hear sea lions barking from their tanks in the lab. *So close*, she thought.

The engine roared to life, the back tires spinning as they caught the pea gravel, spitting up bits as the car raced for the exit. Taillights flashed as the fertility specialist took the last turn before leaving the long single lane entrance to the marine lab.

50.

Noah sat quietly with his hands flat on his thighs, watching the bustle of doctors, nurses and medical technicians as he sat outside the hospital room. Taylor seemed jumpy, but excited as she shifted around in her seat. Noah's mom and Taylor's dad sat quietly talking on a couch stuffed in the corner against a far wall. There was a hint of bleach in the long corridor, making Taylor think of all the things that might have happened in the darkened hospital rooms lining the wall. It wasn't a pleasant thought. The group stood up and stepped closer when the doctor approached. He was tall with an easy smile, his long white coat pristinely matching his perfectly straight teeth.

"Can I see my mom?" Taylor asked. "Is she going to be okay?"

The doctor gave Taylor's shoulder a reassuring pat. "She's doing well, her vitals have stabilized, which is one of the first hurdles. Why don't you go see her while I talk to your dad?"

"Can my friend come?" Taylor asked, pointing to Noah.

Noah felt the doctor's gaze appraise him; he could sense a hesitation, but then the man waved them on.

Taylor knocked on the large white door before pushing it open, Noah trailing behind.

The hospital bed seemed to engulf Taylor's mother, her petite body looking frail in the pale blue paisley hospital gown, a tube connecting an IV to her arm, but she brightened when she saw the two of them.

"Hey guys," Her raspy whisper punctuated her exhaustion, but her eyes twinkled with a loving emotion. "Have a seat, Noah," she said, pointing to a chair perched in the corner of the room. "I'm so glad you came to see me. I never got a chance to thank you." Then she looked at her daughter warmly. "To thank both of you for—"

"Mom," Taylor interrupted, "we have so many questions. Dad said you might be in trouble, might be going away for a while. What does that mean?"

"There's going to be an investigation. But I'll be fine," she told Taylor, her brave smile doing a poor job of hiding the fear in her eyes. Then she shifted her gaze to Noah, her brow creased, eyes filled with tears begging to spill over. "I should have realized—" Kate's throat closed up as she tried to gain control of her emotions. "I didn't know what Dr. Stafford was doing, but there were signs. I should have listened to my intuition, but I was too focused on my work. Too focused on him helping me with my own project. I didn't know he—"

"Listen," Noah jumped in. "I'm fine. In fact, I think I'm great. I know I'm not the only one out there with some

. . . uh . . . differences. Like those creatures out there in the ocean. I think I can help them. I'm not saying all of this is fantastic," he said, holding up his hands to make his point, "but I'm okay with it. Being a freak comes with some perks." A smile lit up Noah's face.

Taylor's mom laughed; its sound made the air seem cleaner somehow.

"And what's the point in whining, right?" Taylor offered. "Evolutionary shifts happen all the time."

The lightness in the room shut off with that statement, like someone had pulled the curtains, blocking out the sun. They all exchanged a knowing glance. As much as Kate wanted to believe Noah was okay with his newfound abilities, she knew something beyond the world's comprehension was now unlocked and she was uncertain about where it would lead.

Noah heard a soft knock on the door behind him, and turned to see a police detective entering the room. "I'm detective Gomez, Dr. Borcelli. I have a few questions, if you don't mind." He glanced at Taylor and Noah.

"Ready to go, Aquaboy?" Taylor quipped.

"Don't call me that." Noah retorted, giving her a light shove and hiding a smile at the new nickname, "or I'll make up a creepy sidekick name for you."

"Thanks again, both of you. This shouldn't take long," Taylor's mom said. "And Taylor, try not to get into any trouble out there."

"Who me?" Taylor said, a wicked smile accentuating her dimples.

Kate sighed deeply as the door shut; she could hear them both laughing as they left the room.

***

"Mind if I sit?" Detective Gomez unbuttoned his coat, clearing his throat before taking a seat in the chair opposite from Kate. "Like you said, this shouldn't take long." He flipped open a notebook and jotted down the date and time. "We have Dr. Stafford at headquarters. He seems to be cooperating, but I had a few additional questions."

Kate gave him an encouraging smile.

"Dr. Borcelli, do you know a scientist named Dr. Diane Fields."

"Yes. The fertility specialist," Kate said. "She helped us when we were trying to have a baby. And she worked with—"

"With Noah's mother, Cheryl Stark, correct?"

"Yes." Kate looked pained. "She recommended her after—"

"After what?"

"Cheryl wanted to have a baby. She was alone, no husband, but she still wanted a family. She went to the fertility clinic, to Dr. Fields. They helped her conceive. We were so excited, my husband and I. We'd been struggling to have a baby for years, and it happened so quickly for her. We went to see her and we got pregnant right away. Noah and Taylor are only six months apart. They're like brother and sister. What does she have to do with my project at the lab?"

"There seems to be information your daughter obtained on your computer. It mentions Dr. Fields."

"I don't know what—"

"Can you tell me about the Trident Initiative?"

Kate face was clouded with confusion. "That's the same thing Noah brought up in the cave," she said softly.

"Dr. Borcelli—"

"Please. Call me Kate."

"Kate," Detective Gomez said, taking a moment to shift in his chair, "Jake Stafford said that he and Dr. Fields were trying to change the genetic complexity of the human race."

"What are you all talking about? My work involved communication, with marine life. We were working on a breakthrough using CRISPR technology, a type of gene editing that—" Kate's eyes filled with understanding. "Oh my God."

"Can you explain to me how this CRISPR technology works?"

"It's a way for people to rewrite an organism's DNA," Kate explained in a flat monotone. "CRISPR is short for Clustered Regularly Interspaced Short Palindromic Repeats. You can search a DNA strand for the right RNA sequence, cut that area, and the endonuclease makes a repair with the edited information. It's a targeted way to alter the genetic code, and it's a simple breakthrough in technology.

"They were using that technology, weren't they? On fetuses?" Kate took a hitching breath in, covering her mouth with a quivering hand. "On our babies?"

Detective Gomez looked solemnly at his hands before continuing. "I'll be honest, Kate. I've known Jake Stafford for years now, and I've always thought of him as a smart guy, but if he's involved in this, he's probably pushed it beyond what anyone could imagine. Unfortunately, it looks like the files were wiped clean. We have an IT guy on it; he's trying to access the hard drive, but do you have any other information about this?"

Kate wiped a tear from her eye. "Taylor said he was talking about evidence on the boat. Getting rid of evidence." She pointed to a journal on the side table near her bed. "My notes are in there. But I don't think it will have anything of use, outside of my own work."

"Do you mind if I take this to review?"

"Of course."

"I'm sorry to put you through this, Dr. Borcelli. I'll get this back to you. And we appreciated your cooperation. We may have more questions after we—"

A soft knock interrupted them, and Taylor rushed into the room.

Noah stood beside her, watching in amazement as she fumbled with one of the soggy backpacks on the linoleum floor, mumbling to herself as she searched through its contents.

"It's on here," Taylor shouted, holding up her plastic-baggie wrapped digital recorder. "It was that day that you were out on the research boat, that day you say you let Bessy go, remember?" Kate nodded.

"I was in the lab because we didn't have school that day and I heard Doc Stafford yelling from the other room. He was on the speaker phone, yelling about the project. I thought he was talking about your work with the seals, but I just listened to it again. It's more than that. It's right here."

Noah looked at his friend with a smile, and she beamed at him before continuing to unwind the bands and pull out the device from the watertight baggy. She flipped through the recorder's digital files until she found the one she wanted.

Noah touched his friend's shoulder, trying to calm her down. "But Tay, it sounds like this puts your mom with that other fertility doctor and Doc Stafford."

"But that's just it, Noah! My mom was gone. Miles out to sea. And Doc Stafford is yelling at someone on the phone about the initiative. How my mom was going to screw it all up because she wasn't in the loop. He called her clueless about it. A liability."

Taylor placed the recorder on the table top, pushing the other contents aside so it sat alone on the metal surface.

"Listen," she said. "The creepy stuff was all Doc Stafford's idea."

51.

Three months later, Jake Stafford sat next to his attorney, all smiles. His thick brown hair was slicked back, his chiseled features striking in a dark grey Armani suit, the maroon shirt accentuating his green eyes. He turned around and smiled at the group of people behind him who were assembled in the courtroom, then glanced at the jury, feeling more like a celebrity than a defendant.

During the past several weeks, Jake Stafford had become a household name; his picture splashed on the front pages of national newspapers and cable news shows, with lawmakers, scientists and public officials chiming in about the ethics of genetic engineering. What excited him most was the focus on climate change as the impetus for his work. He thought, "Finally, people are getting it."

His lawyer sat stoically beside Stafford, reviewing his notes.

Jake turned his attention to the judge, an attractive woman in her 50s. He was so confident he nearly winked at her, but caught himself, a devious grin spreading across his face. "This is going to be a piece of cake," he whispered to the tall man jotting notes.

"I'd advise you to stay quiet during the proceedings, Mr. Stafford," the tall man whispered to his client.

Stafford bristled at being chastised. "It's *Doctor* Stafford, counselor."

The lawyer adjusted his glasses, his eyes blank as he studied his client. Then without comment, he returned to his notebook.

The prosecuting attorney, a stocky man with a dark blue three-piece suit and graying brown hair, stood to call his first witness. "I call Dr. Diane Fields to the stand."

Stafford whipped around in his chair. He watched as Diane Fields entered the room, dressed in a white linen suit, hair tied up in a tight bun, glasses resting perfectly on an aquiline nose. He glared at her, conveying a burning thought: *We had an agreement.*

Dr. Fields refused to look at Jake as she raised her right hand to be sworn in. From the back of the courtroom, a small green light on Taylor's new digital recorder shown brightly, noting that the device was working. She stuffed it silently back into her pocket and leaned over to Noah, whispering, "Well, this ought to be good."

Taylor's dad gave her a nudge to remind her to stay quiet.

The prosecuting attorney stepped up to the witness stand. "Dr. Fields, can you please explain to the jury what your specialty is."

"I'm a geneticist, with a specialty in infertility."

"And you work at a fertility clinic here in Santiempo?"

"It's actually in Scott Creek, northeast of Santiempo, but yes."

"And can you explain the type of cases you were involved in?"

Dr. Fields cleared her throat and adjusted her glasses, before responding. "I can't give specific information about my clients," she said, her voice cracking a bit, "but in general I helped couples that were having trouble conceiving a child to get pregnant."

"And did you help single people conceive as well?"

Dr. Fields looked over at the defense attorney, who was ignoring her as he jotted notes. She leaned into the microphone and responded, "Yes."

The prosecuting attorney returned to his notes, before asking, "And can you explain to the jury how that process works?" He spread his hands and smiled, "I mean it normally does take two, correct?"

A chuckle arose from the audience, and the judge warned them about decorum.

"In cases where single mothers or same sex couples would like to conceive a child, we use donor specimens."

"From a sperm bank, correct?"

"Yes."

"So this process is in a laboratory setting. And involves a set of strict guidelines and regulations, correct?"

"Yes."

"Dr. Fields, have you ever heard of the genetic editing technique called CRISPR?"

"I have."

"Was this a technique that you utilized in the past?"

"I did some work at the marine lab with Katherine Borcelli."

"On what, specifically?"

"She was working on ways to affect communication in marine mammals, to alter the brain's receptors to facilitate communication and also to focus on creating a specimen who could survive severe water pollution. We performed experimentation on embryos to facilitate a change using this technology that can alter a DNA strand."

"I'm sorry, Dr. Fields," the man said, leaning onto the witness stand, "but can you be more specific?" He returned to the files on his desk, flipping through pages before reading, "According to this document, you had been involved in genetic manipulation of thirty-five California sea lion and harbor seal embryos, and you and Dr. Borcelli were tracking changes in development." He looked over at Dr. Fields. "Is that correct?"

She looked at the jury before responding. "Yes."

"And for the purposes of educating the jury on why this might be important, can you explain your reasoning for this manipulation?"

"Seals were dying," Dr. Fields said loudly. "Each year the oceans are becoming more polluted, the mercury levels are rising. We tried to fight on the environmental front, but it seemed futile." She looked out at the people in the gallery, searching for any sign that the audience was on her side. "Kate and I were friends from college. Always doing recycling drives, protests at corporations who polluted our waters, but it didn't matter. There are islands of garbage floating in our waters!" she said, her voice reaching a more fevered pitch. "Garbage and metals are killing our ecology."

"So," the prosecuting attorney said, "if you couldn't fix the environment, you thought you could fix the things that lived in it?"

The defense attorney continued to jot notes, never raising his eyes, but objected, saying, "Leading the witness."

"I retract the question," the prosecutor said, returning to his notes. "And this work with Dr. Borcelli was limited to seals and sea lions, correct?"

"Yes."

"And is this experimentation still going on?"

"No. We stopped after—"

"After what?"

"After one of the births nearly a year ago," Dr. Fields whispered into the microphone. "It was a failure."

"How so?"

"Massive deformations: abnormalities in the skull structure, the skeletal structure, growth patterns."

"Aside from the outward appearance, was this creature a normal functioning specimen?"

"Yes, I would say so, although Kate—um—Dr. Borcelli would be better able to answer that."

"And what happened to this 'failure'?"

"Dr. Borcelli released it."

"Locally?"

"Yes, that's my understanding."

"Can you tell me if genetic manipulation was limited to just marine life, Dr. Fields?"

She once again looked for any feedback from the defense attorney. Nothing.

"I can't speak about specific clients at the clinic."

"Well, let me refresh your memory then," the man said. He turned several pages, before stopping at one specific document. "Can you confirm that Dr. Jacob Stafford visited your clinic fifteen times during the month of July in 2002, fifteen years ago?"

"I would have to check my records."

"They're right here," the man said, handing a folder in to evidence. "Please mark these as exhibit C."

"Again, can you confirm that Dr. Stafford regularly worked with you at your clinic?"

"Yes," she said.

"And were these embryos ever manipulated prior to insemination?"

"He said he found a way, the answer."

"Shut up, Diane!" Stafford yelled from the defense table. The judge banged the gavel to quiet the court.

"And tell me, Dr. Fields, is this type of genetic manipulation being utilized in human embryos?"

Jake stood up in his chair, yelling, "Objection!"

"Sit down, Dr. Stafford," the judge warned. "Counselor, please advise your client to be quiet or I'll cite him with contempt."

Jake sat down, smoothing his suit jacket and firing daggers of hatred toward Dr. Fields.

"Dr. Fields," the prosecuting attorney continued, "you have come here to testify with the understanding that you will gain immunity from any future prosecution regarding this matter, correct?"

"Objection!" Jake called out again.

The judge pounded her gavel sharply and looked over her glasses at Jake. "This is your final warning, Dr. Stafford. You are trying my patience."

The prosecutor looked at Jake as if to say, "May I continue?" Then he turned back to the witness.

"Can you tell me, Dr. Fields, if you were ever involved in using CRISPR on human embryos?"

"Yes," she said quietly. "In a way."

"How so?" he asked.

"I gave access to the embryos for the research."

"Access to whom?"

Dr. Fields pointed across the room at Jake Stafford.

"And when was this?"

"Fifteen years ago."

"And tell me. What was the outcome of these experiments?"

"We thought it was a failure, and I thought we had moved on."

"But Dr. Stafford had not moved on, is that correct?"

"Yes." Diane Fields' eyes bounced from her lap to the jury, then back to her tightly clasped hands in her lap.

"How was he continuing this research?"

Dr. Fields looked at the defense attorney and the judge, wondering whether she had to answer the question. The attorney next to Stafford continued to ignore her. She could see beads of sweat break out on Stafford's upper lip.

The judge said, "You can answer the question, Dr. Fields."

"He has been watching them. Waiting. And he said it finally paid off."

Dr. Fields was crying, and the prosecutor handed her a tissue. "He said he thought we could change the course of evolution. Fix things so when the world's environment changed, we'd be ready. Life on land will become unbearable. Sea level rise. Increases in flooding, drought, destructive weather patterns, famine. Evolving back to the oceans would be a better solution. When he told me what he was doing with the failures … I didn't know he'd kill—"

Stafford stood up, shouting, "Shut up! She's lying!"

"Sit down Doctor Stafford!" the judge ordered.

Tears rolled down Dr. Fields' face and the prosecutor handed her a tissue. "I never wanted to hurt anyone," she continued as she dabbed the corners of her eyes.

"Tell me, Dr. Fields, was Kate Borcelli ever involved in manipulation of human embryos with you and Dr. Stafford?"

"No. Just the seals and sea lions. It was Jake's idea with the human embryos at the clinic," she continued, her voice growing more strained as she talked, tears coursing down her face. "I just thought we could help things along. I never knew he was following them, tracking them, and . . . How could you just kill innocent children?" she screamed across the room. "Why didn't you just leave it alone?"

Stafford jumped up again from behind the table, and screamed at the jury, "A scientist can't be considered a genius when there are rejects!"

The judge was banging his gavel, calling for order.

Stafford stood tall, composing himself, smoothing a long strand of hair that had fallen out of place, and adjusting his tie, like he was at the lecture podium. "You can't have successful evolutionary change without destroying the defective specimens," he said quietly, as if talking to a bunch of children. "It defeats the purpose."

His condescending smile at the people gathered in the courtroom finished his sentence: *You morons.*

52.

The following week, the beaches were open again and life had basically returned to normal for Taylor and Noah. They spent hours after school in the chilly waters beyond Natural Bridges, Noah swimming freely with Taylor at his side in full scuba gear; she had yet to realize all of Noah's abilities. "Girls mature differently," she'd say every time she'd pop to the surface of the water.

With each dive, they were greeted by dolphins, an occasional stingray, and harbor seals that circled and twirled around them as they explored the ocean depths. Word soon spread around school about Noah's abilities. At first Noah heard the whispers that had haunted him his entire childhood echo off the walls outside of class, but he no longer cared.

Since he discovered what he could do in the ocean three months ago, he had gone out on research vessels with the local marine biologists and had helped them rescue four sea lion pups, worked with a pod of dolphins to find a floating mass of plastic and garbage that had been floating for years, entangling birds and fish, and last week he had helped a wayward humpback whale and her calf return to the ocean after becoming stranded in a northern inlet.

Noah got to swim with the pod of whales for miles as they sung alongside him. The local papers called him a hero.

He was learning to master the differences in how each species communicated and could now free dive for 15 minutes without taking a breath.

Once school started again, Noah walked proudly through the halls, his fingers flexing and retracting as if to ward off any potential attackers, and he smiled when he saw the look of wonder some kids gave him as he passed by, thinking, "I never thought being a freak of nature could be so much fun."

Several weeks after he returned to school, six kids he knew his whole life but never talked to before came up to him, forming a tight semi-circle around him: "Can you really swim without scuba gear? Did you really swim around a humpback whale? Can you talk to seals?"

Noah stood quietly as he was peppered with questions and answered each one with certainty, his voice never wavering—even when hecklers would scream out obscenities at him from farther down the hall. He simply acknowledged them with a grin before continuing his explanations.

One boy, who was new to the school and very shy, approached Noah after his math class one day. He had tousled hair and soft amber eyes that darted nervously from side to side. His shoulders stayed slumped in a heavy dark blue pullover sweatshirt like the ones Noah always used to wear. The boy's hands were stuffed deeply in the center pocket, pulling it down in a V-shape over the front of his jeans.

"Can you really talk to seals?" the boy asked quietly, his gaze firmly focused on Noah's webbed fingers. Noah didn't mind people looking at his hands anymore, and simply nodded as the boy examined him. "Yep," he said.

The boy pulled his own hands from his pockets and held them out straight in front of Noah, turning them ever so slightly as he whispered, "You think I can talk to them, too?"

The tiny pale hands twisted back and forth near Noah's waist, the webbing between the fingers nearly translucent as the boy opened and closed his fists. Noah was no longer surprised when he met a new kid with the malady. Over the past weeks, two boys and three girls had approached him with a similar question, all of them twisting and flexing hands that mirrored his own.

Noah smiled broadly until the boy met his gaze.

"Come on," Noah said as he placed his arm around the younger boy's shoulder. "I have some other kids I want you to meet."

ABOUT THE AUTHOR

J. Finn Wake has always been drawn to the water. As a child, she dreamed of being a mermaid. As a young woman, she swam with seals in the Sea of Cortez and snorkeled with sea turtles and schools of fish off the shores of Hawaii, always in constant wonder as she interacted with the marine life. Over the years, she has written and published hundreds of feature articles for regional magazines and newspapers, as well as essays in the *Cup of Comfort* series. She is currently the editor of a weekly newspaper and lives with her husband and two teenage sons in the San Francisco Bay Area. This is her first novel.

Follow her on Twitter @jfinnwake or visit her online at www.jfinnwake.com.